ONE MORE NIGHT WITH THE FROGS

Benny Tate

RIVERSTONE GROUP

PUBLISHING

Dedication

This book is dedicated to the two most important people in my life: my wife Barbara and my daughter Savannah Abigail.

Barbara and I met in a doctor's office in Tracy City, Tennessee; but I know the "Great Physician" arranged our meeting. She is my very best friend, loving companion, and soul mate. I still can't figure out why she married me, but I thank God she did. If she leaves me, I'm going with her.

Savannah Abigail is the joy of my life. Her name *Abigail* literally means "her father's joy," and she has been a joy to me. It has been said, "Children make a rich man poor"; but in my case, "Savannah has made a poor man rich." She has wonderfully enriched my life. I am honored to be her father.

Contents

Acknowledgements

To Tammy Cochran for the countless hours spent in front of a computer, typing and retyping the manuscript. Her suggestions and encouragement were indispensable to the finished product. My name is on the front of this book but truly hers should be also because I never would have attempted this book without her assistance in typing and editing.

To Medora Pelt, a "Grammar Hammer" who has helped my pulpit ministry and my writing.

To Rock Springs Congregational Methodist Church for allowing me to pastor the greatest people in the world for many years.

To Clayton Jones for believing in me more than I believe in myself.

To the memory of Don Mason, Don Wisdom, and Joe and Rennice Roberts.

To my mother Melba Williams and sister Rhonda Gibbs who I love in a special way.

To my in-laws Jim and Stella Roberts for always treating me fairly and with respect.

To Vicki, Kevin, Mike, Terry, and Donna who I have not known long but love deeply.

To my church staff — Stan, Cameron, Renee, and Deb — thanks for all they do to make me look better.

Last and most importantly, I owe everything to Jesus Christ, my Savior and Lord. He saved me and put my feet on solid ground and gave me a life worth living. For all this and more, I will be grateful for all eternity.

Foreword

Anyone who meets Benny Tate knows immediately that he is an original. He has wit, charm, and a positive outlook on life. Although he has experienced a few tragedies along the way, he has maintained an unsinkable spirit.

Benny also possesses a keen insight. In this book, he shares many of his observations and insights; and they are loaded with humor. You will find yourself laughing one minute and crying the next.

It is an honor to call Benny my friend, and I highly recommend *One More Night with the Frogs*.

— John C. Maxwell
Founder
INJOY Group

ISBN 0-9706117-1-4

Design and Production
Riverstone Group, LLC, Canton, Georgia

Printed in the United States of America

Scripture quotations are from the King James Bible.

CHAPTER ONE

One More Night with the Frogs

A biblical story that has often fascinated and intrigued me is found in Exodus 8:1-13. The Hebrews had been slaves to the Egyptians for more than four centuries; but God's plan for His people, the Hebrews, was to escape the dictatorial leadership of the Pharaoh of Egypt. God chose a man named Moses to lead His people out of this bondage and tyranny.

God sent Moses to Pharaoh's palace on three different occasions. Each time he instructed Pharaoh, "Let my people go." The third time he issued an interesting ultimatum, saying, "Either you let my people go, or God will send vast hordes of frogs across your entire land from one border to the other." Pharaoh didn't listen; however, God did just as He said. Frogs were everywhere: in their beds, in their cooking pots, and in their bathtubs!

Interestingly enough, frogs could not be killed because they were an object of worship in Egypt. This is similar to people worshipping cows in India. People there are starving to death but worshipping the beef stock. Did you know that in India rats eat twenty percent of the food supply? But by no means would they kill the rats because Hinduism teaches reincarnation, and that rat just might be "Uncle Harry."

Finally, after much discomfort, Pharaoh summoned Moses and his brother Aaron and begged Moses, "Plead with your Lord to take the frogs away from me and my people." Moses replied, "You set the time! Tell me when you want the frogs gone." I will forever be intrigued by Pharaoh's answer. Realizing God could have removed all of the frogs instantly, Pharaoh said, "Take them all away — tomorrow." He simply wanted ONE MORE NIGHT WITH THE FROGS.

I am convinced many of us are like Pharaoh. There are many things in our lives God wants to eradicate; but we have a tendency to want to hold on to them instead of letting go. In turn, we spend ONE MORE NIGHT WITH THE FROGS.

WE HAD RATHER SPEND ONE
MORE NIGHT WITH THE FROGS
THAN DEAL WITH OUR SIN.

The Bible teaches in 2 Corinthians 6:2 that: ". . . now is the day of salvation." The Bible also teaches us in Proverbs 28:13 that God wants you and me to confess and forsake our sin. But many times we have a tendency to continue in our sin and to spend time with the frogs — even though God desires us to be free.

Do you know how captors catch monkeys on the South Sea Islands? They take a coconut and tie it to a tree. The coconut has a small hole cut in it, and rice is placed in the bottom. The monkey smells the rice; therefore, he places his hand into the coconut and makes a fist. Guess what? He can't get his fist out of the hole! What is more amazing, however, is if he would just let go of the rice he would be free! But he will not; therefore, he is captured.

Perhaps there is something in our hand that is keeping us from freedom. The Bible says, "If the Son therefore shall make you free, ye shall be free indeed" (John 8:36). Would we rather spend ONE MORE NIGHT WITH THE FROGS than deal with our sin?

WE HAD RATHER SPEND ONE
MORE NIGHT WITH THE FROGS
THAN DEAL WITH OUR STRESS.

I was recently shopping at Southlake Mall in Morrow, Georgia, when I spoke to a lady as I entered a store. After we exchanged greetings, I asked, "How are you?" She immediately said as she jerked her shoulders back: "Honey, I am too blessed to be stressed!" And she was correct. God's children have no reason to go around stressed out. We serve the Prince of Peace. (Isaiah 9:6) I am of deep conviction that many times people enjoy being "all stressed up with nowhere to go."

A man was having severe headaches, shortness of breath, acute pain in his neck, and reoccurring dizzy spells. After a thorough examination by his physician, he was given the devastating news that he only had six months to live. His physician encouraged him to "live it up" and enjoy the last few months on this earth.

"Buy a new car, a new house, or a new wardrobe," he suggested. The man decided to get a tailored suit. While being fitted for his shirt, the tailor told the man he needed a size 16. The man said, "No, I wear a size 14." Again, the tailor said he needed a size 16. By this time, the man was getting upset and abruptly shouted, "For the last time, I wear a size 14!" The tailor quietly responded, "Sir, you can have a size 14; but you will have severe headaches, shortness of breath, acute pain in your neck, and reoccurring dizzy spells." Some people had rather spend ONE MORE NIGHT WITH THE FROGS than deal with their stress.

WE HAD RATHER SPEND ONE MORE NIGHT WITH THE FROGS THAN DEAL WITH OUR STRIFE.

I recently read about a lady who was ninety-four years old when she died. She was an old maid who never had one single date. She gave some unique but specific instructions to the funeral director that would be handling her arrangements. She demanded that she have no male pallbearers. Her reason was: "They would not take me out while I was living, and I sure don't want them to take me out when I'm dead."

This elderly lady no doubt went to her grave with strife in her heart toward men. Many people today are experiencing the same feeling, yet they never try to reconcile the relationship with the person or persons they have disgruntled feelings toward — even though the Bible commands this of us. They had rather live with the wrong attitude than live as a Christian. I realize there are some people you can't reconcile with, but that really isn't even the issue. The issue is one you must ask yourself: "Have I earnestly tried to reconcile?" We can't determine what happens TO us, but we can determine what happens IN us. Go and try. Or would you rather spend ONE MORE NIGHT WITH THE FROGS than deal with your strife?

WE HAD RATHER SPEND ONE MORE NIGHT WITH THE FROGS THAN DEAL WITH OUR SERVICE.

Did you know God has gifted all of His children and we all have at least one special service to do? The number of people who say, "I want to do something, but I just don't know what God wants me to do," amazes me. Do you really believe God wants to keep His will a mystery from His children?

I am a father. I have one daughter named Savannah Abigail. Before Savannah, I would travel and preach a message titled "Ten Steps to Raising the Healthy, Productive, Godly Child." Then along came Savannah Abigail. I revised my message. It became "Three Things You May Want to Try Because They May or May Not Work." I assure you I don't want my will to be a mystery to my child. And I am convinced God doesn't want His will to be a mystery to His children either.

Many times we use this attitude as a cop-out for doing nothing for Christ and His Kingdom. Three questions that should be asked when you are trying to locate your area of service (giftedness):
1. What am I good at doing? (include opinions of others)
2. What do I enjoy doing?
3. What do I do that gets compliments from others?
Scores of people are spending ONE MORE NIGHT WITH THE FROGS and not dealing with their service.

WE HAD RATHER SPEND ONE
MORE NIGHT WITH THE FROGS
THAN DEAL WITH OUR SCARS.

I once heard someone say, "If you treat everyone you meet as if they are hurting, you will be treating ninety percent of the people you meet correctly." People no doubt carry a lot of scars. They have scars of divorce, neglect, abandonment, emotional hurt, and physical pain. The list goes on and on. I can't explain why bad things happen, but I do know what God wants us to do after they happen. He wants us to use our circumstances to help others rather than internalize them. The Bible teaches in 2 Corinthians 1:4: "Who comforteth us in all our tribulation, that we may be able to comfort them which are in any trouble."

The scars of life can make us bitter or better. They can make us caring and compassionate or cold and calloused. The same sun that hardens the clay melts the ice. The choice is yours. You can reflect on the scars or reach for the stars.

I was nearly thirty before I met my biological father. He was a professional gambler who traveled all over the world and gambled with some of the biggest names in the industry, but he wasn't much of a father. There is a great difference in fathering a child and being a father to a child.

Every child needs a father. I can remember as a boy longing to use the word "Daddy." I would see other children with their dads, and I longed to have a relationship with mine.

Finally, because of the efforts of my sister Rhonda, I met my dad in a restaurant in Nashville, Tennessee. He apologized to me. He said how sorry he was for never being there for me. He then shared with me that he was now a Christian and asked me to pray for him. After I prayed, he said something I will never forget: "Son, we didn't spend anytime here on Earth together; but because we both know Christ, we can spend eternity together." He died not long after that meeting. I look forward to getting to know him one day in Heaven.

Am I bitter toward my dad? No. I share my story all over America simply to help others who are going through similar circumstances. Rick Warren, author of *The Purpose Driven Church*, said, "It is wise to learn from experience, but it is wiser to learn from the experience of others." I desire to learn from the sad experience with my father and be a greater father to my daughter. I had rather deal with my scars than spend ONE MORE NIGHT WITH THE FROGS.

WE HAD RATHER SPEND ONE
MORE NIGHT WITH THE FROGS
THAN DEAL WITH OUR SOMEDAY.

I have learned that "one of these days" is usually "none of these days." I talk to people all of the time who are someday going to get in church, start doing ministry, start tithing and construct a budget, or go on a diet and start exercising. But the sad reality is they had rather spend ONE MORE NIGHT WITH THE FROGS than deal with their someday.

Thomas Carlyle was a Scottish essayist and poet who late in life married his secretary, Jane Welch. She was the daughter of a prominent doctor. Not long after they married, they found she had terminal cancer.

Carlyle was a famous man in his day. He traveled the world, presenting his work to large, adoring crowds. When he was home, he focused only on his writing, therefore, not seeing his wife for days on end.

The months passed and eventually Jane died. She was buried in a country cemetery not far from their home. After the funeral, several friends gathered at the Carlyle home. He appreciated their friendship but eventually needed to be alone. He excused himself and walked up the stairs to Jane's bedroom. He sat down in a chair next to her bed. He noticed a book on her nightstand, and he began reading it. It was her diary. She had written: "He came by today, and it was like Heaven to me! I love him so." He continued reading. When he came to the last page where she obviously was too weak to even be writing, he read her last words: "The day has grown long, and the shadows are up the hall. I have not heard his footsteps. I know he will not be coming by today. Oh, how I wish I could tell him 'I love him'."

Carlyle's friends were startled when he dashed passed them out the door. One of them said, "The cemetery! Maybe he's gone to the cemetery." They ran to the grave where she was buried just hours earlier. There indeed was Thomas Carlyle. He was lying on the fresh, wet dirt of his wife's grave. He was pounding his fist on the ground saying, "If I had only known!"

The visit you have been planning to make, make it. The gift you have been planning to give, give it. The call you have been planning, do it. The words you have been planning to say, say them. Do it now! We certainly are NOT promised "someday."

CHAPTER TWO

How to Develop a Good Attitude

Philippians 2:1-5

1. If *there be* therefore any consolation in Christ,
   if any comfort of love, if any fellowship of the Spirit, if
   any bowels and mercies,
2. Fulfil ye my joy, that ye be likeminded, having the
   same love, *being* of one accord, of one mind.
3. Let nothing be *done* through strife or vainglory; but in
   lowliness of mind let each esteem other better than
   themselves.
4. Look not every man on his own things, but every man
   also on the things of others.
5. Let this mind be in you, which was also in Christ Jesus.

The Bible teaches us we are to strive to have the mind or attitude of Christ. (Philippians 2:5) It also explains the type of attitude He possesses. (Philippians 2:3-4) Our attitude is so vital because every action — whether it be good or bad — stems from our attitude.

Chuck Swindoll said, "Attitude, to me, is more important

than the facts. It is more important than the past, than education, than money, than circumstances, than failures, than success, than what other people think, say, or do." It is more important than appearance, giftedness, or skill. It will make or break a company, church, or home. How is your attitude concerning your mate, job, school, friends, mother-in-law?

A man walked into a restaurant and asked the waitress, "Do you serve crabs?" She quickly responded, "We serve everybody. Just sit down."

Two men were drinking their morning coffee when one asked the other: "Did you wake up grumpy this morning?" His reply: "No, I let her sleep."

Our attitude is an inward feeling expressed by outward behavior. Attitude is tremendously important. I am convinced there are three reasons we need a proper attitude.

First, it determines our approach to life. Many people believe circumstances determine their approach to life. The Bible is very clear that circumstances do not. Remember Paul was not in the Ritz-Carlton when he penned these Scriptures. He was in a cold, damp Roman prison, waiting to be executed. His circumstances were not great; however, his attitude was. The principles by which we live will determine the world in which we live.

Secondly, attitude determines our kind of relationships with people. Mark 12:31 says, "Thou shalt love thy neighbour as thyself." We tend to place all of the focus on "love thy neighbour" when the truth is we cannot really love our neighbor until we love ourselves. We need a proper attitude concerning ourselves. We must love who we are.

A man involved in an automobile accident jumped out of his car. He was irate toward the lady with whom he had collided. He began yelling, "Can't you drive? You ought to watch where you're going!" He then said, "You're the fourth car that has hit me today!"

I know scores of people who cannot get along with their families or people at work, at church, and/or at school. Many times, however, others are not the problem. The problem is a rotten attitude.

The third reason it is so important is our attitude many times determines our success or failure. Paul said, "I can do all things through Christ which strengtheneth me" (Philippians 4:13). He had a positive attitude.

There's the story of two shoe salesmen who were sent to an island to sell shoes. Upon arrival, the first salesman was shocked to realize no one wore shoes. He immediately sent a telegram to his home office in Chicago saying, "Will return tomorrow. No one here wears shoes." The second salesman was thrilled by the same realization. He immediately wired the home office saying, "Please send me 10,000 pairs of shoes. Everyone here needs them!"

I am not naive enough to think attitude is all you need in life. Neither do I think just having a good attitude will make me able to play basketball like Michael Jordan, skate like Nancy Kerrigan, or golf like Tiger Woods. I do believe, however, if a proper attitude is maintained, whatever is done in life will be done better.

Now that we have established the fact concerning the importance of our attitude, the next step is to develop a good one. Allow
me to share five principles that have been very beneficial to me.

The first principle to developing a good attitude is *to take
God at His word.* According to Romans 8:28, "All things work
together for good to them that love God." God said He is working all things for the good of His children. Whether we are sick
or well, promoted or demoted, rich or poor, single or married, He
is watching out for our well-being.

In 1998, I purchased the nicest car I have ever owned. It was
a gorgeous, new, white Buick Le Sabre. Up to this point, I had
only owned small fuel-efficient automobiles. I never experienced
much comfort during my travels to speaking engagements.

A month after purchasing my dream car, I went to speak at a
revival in Edgefield, South Carolina. I can't express how much I
enjoyed the trip. My back wasn't sore and my legs weren't cramp-
ing like I experienced when driving the other cars. That night I
preached the message titled "How All Things Work Together for
Good to Those Who Love the Lord." Everything was going great!

The next evening before church, I was eating at a small diner
with one of the families from the church. While there, it started
to rain. The rain intensified and turned to hail the size of grape-
fruits. I can't describe the pains I experienced each time a ball
dinged my precious car. My windshield was broken in four different places. In the end, there were only a few places on my new
vehicle that were not dented.

After the horrible storm had passed, I went out to inspect the damage. It was all I could do not to cry. (I really believe I would have if it would have helped the situation.) While viewing my car, a lady who had been at the revival the night before walked up. Seeing how upset I looked, she said, "Remember, all things work together for good to them that love the Lord." I just wanted to slap her (in Jesus' Name, of course)! I'm only kidding. She was correct. Rain or shine, storm or serenity, we are to take God at His word. Charles Spurgeon said, "God is too loving to be unkind, too wise to be mistaken; and when we can't trace His hand, we can trust His heart."

The second principle to developing a good attitude is *to choose to have one.* A good attitude occurs not by chance but by choice. We can either wake up in the morning and say, "Good morning, Lord" or "Good Lord, it's morning." Abraham Lincoln said, "I am as happy as I make up my mind to be."

One of my favorite stories is the one about the boy named Jeb. Every morning his mother would come into his room at 5:30 to wake him. She would say, "Jeb, it's going to be a great day!" It was Jeb's job every day to go outside first thing and get coal to start the fire to heat the house. He hated this job. So hearing his mother say what a great day it would be was not what he wanted to hear.

One day she came in as usual and said, "It's going to be a great day!" when Jeb snapped back saying, "No, Mom. It's not going to be a great day. It's going to be a lousy day! I'm tired. The house is cold, and I don't want to get up to get the coal." She replied, "I didn't know you felt that way, sweetheart. Why don't you go back to bed and get some sleep." Jeb thought to himself: *Why didn't I think of this long before now?*

He woke up two hours later. The house was warm, and he could smell breakfast cooking. He rolled out of bed, put his clothes on, and went to the kitchen. "Boy, am I hungry," he said. "I am well rested, and breakfast is cooked. This is great." "Sweetheart," his mother said, "you don't get any food today. Remember how you said it was going to be a terrible day? Well, as your mother, I am going to do my best to make it terrible for you. You go back to bed and stay there all day. You are not allowed to come out or to eat. I'll see you tomorrow morning at 5:30."

Jeb dejectedly walked back to his room and got into bed. He was able to sleep for only about an hour more since there is just so much sleep one can get. He spent the day moping around his room, getting hungrier and hungrier. When it finally got dark, he went back to bed, waiting for morning. He woke up hours before daylight and put on his clothes. He was sitting on the edge of his bed when his mother opened the door. Before she could say a word, Jeb jumped up and said, "Mom, it's going to be a great day!" What was true for Jeb is also true for us. We can change our attitude because it is our choice.

The third principle to developing a good attitude is *to think right*. We need to do a "checkup from the neck up" and get rid of "stinking thinking." "Whatsoever things are true, whatsoever things are honest, whatsoever things are just, whatsoever things are pure, whatsoever things are lovely, whatsoever things are of good report; if there be any virtue, and if there be any praise, think on these things" (Philippians 4:8). The fearful, negative, and depressive thoughts you have do not come from God. "God hath not given us the spirit of fear" (2 Timothy 1:7). Those thoughts come from the enemy. Therefore, we do have a choice of what we think about.

Who we associate with and what we watch, read, and listen to are vitally important. Have you ever had a thought or picture that seemed to just "pop" in your mind? Well, it didn't. Do you realize that about ninety percent of our mind is subconscious? It stores everything we see, hear, read, or think. That is the reason it is so important that we hear, read, and listen to the proper things. Proverbs 23:7 says it best: "As he thinketh in his heart, so is he."

The fourth principle to developing a good attitude is *to associate with positive people.* Birds of a feather do flock together. Our environment determines our association. Our association determines our attitude. Our attitude determines the decisions we make, and the decisions we make determine the end result of our lives. Charles "Tremendous" Jones says, "Tell me what you are reading and who you are associating with, and I will tell you where you will be five years from now." "He that walketh with wise men shall be wise: but a companion of fools shall be destroyed" (Proverbs 13:20).

A young man and woman were madly in love. They were planning to be married. Before they could wed, the man received news that he was to report immediately to the armed services. He was to serve only for one year. He promised he would write his bride-to-be every day which he did. He sent her 365 letters. That young woman did marry a year later as planned. She married the mailman! Association is extremely important.

The fifth principle to developing a good attitude is *to work at it daily.* Just because we had a good attitude yesterday does not mean we will have a good attitude tomorrow. It is something we must work at every day. I hasten to say it is easier to *maintain* a good attitude than to *regain* a good attitude. That is why it is so important to get in the habit of constantly thinking positive thoughts.

You can have a great attitude because acquiring one is just a habit of the mind and habits can be acquired. Begin using your mind to think positive thoughts today!

A young business executive took some work home to complete for an important meeting the next day. Every few minutes, his five-year-old son would interrupt his chain of thought. After several interruptions, the young executive spotted the evening paper which had a world map on it. He took the map, tore it into many pieces, and told his son to put the map together again. He thought this would keep the boy busy for awhile. To the executive's amazement, however, the boy finished the map in a matter of minutes. Astonished, the executive asked the boy how he did that so quickly. The little boy responded by telling his dad, "There was a picture of a man on the other side; so when I got the man right, the world was right." Needless to say, we can alter our lives simply by getting the man right which often means altering our attitude.

CHAPTER THREE

The Day Jesus Provided Fish and Chips for Everyone

There is only one miracle that Jesus performed which all four of the Gospel writers chose to record. It is the miracle of the feeding of five thousand. (John 6:1-13) Jesus crossed the Sea of Galilee, and a great multitude followed Him to the mountainside. The Bible is clear there were five thousand men. Theologians estimate there could have been as many as fifteen thousand when the women and children were added.

Seeing the great number of people, Jesus said to one of the disciples named Philip: "Where shall we buy bread that these people may eat?" Philip responded, "Eight months' wages would not buy enough bread for each one to have a bite!" Another of His disciples, Andrew, spoke and said, "There is a lad here with five small barley loaves and two small fish. But how far will that go among so many?" Jesus then asked the people to sit down. He took the five small loaves and the two small fish and blessed them so greatly that everyone there had "fish and chips." Everyone was filled, and still there were twelve baskets with fragments of barley loaves left over! I learned three important lessons from this beautiful passage.

I learned first *there is no problem too big for Jesus to solve.* They had a sizeable problem here. You do the math. The quantity of food was very small, and the quality of the food was not the best. Barley loaves were the main course for poor people, and the two fish were like pickled or dried fish or sardines as we know it. With this, they had thousands to feed. I am convinced we all have problems. I have problems, and you have problems; all of God's children have problems. The wonderful truth is *there is no problem too big for Jesus to solve.*

Corrie Ten Boom said, "There is no panic in Heaven — only plans." The Bible says, "With men this is impossible; but with God all things are possible" (Matthew 19:26). We need to quit talking about *im*possible and start talking about *Him* possible. All things are possible through Jesus Christ.

My wife Barbara taught me early in our marriage *there is no problem too big for Jesus to solve.* She and I had dated only a few times when I realized I was in love. You say that is puppy love, and I say it is real to the dogs! We agreed we wanted to be married, but she insisted I ask her dad for her hand in marriage. Shortly after that, I sat down with her dad, Jim Roberts, and shared our plans with him. He was kind but recommended that we not marry. He then explained his reason.

He said, "Benny, you are healthy; Barbara is not. She has epileptic seizures. She has been known to have as many as eight a day — sometimes where blood would gush from her mouth. She has had seizures where she would lose five pounds at a time. She has been to many hospitals, including the Mayo Clinic in Rochester, Minnesota. She was told there is a scar on her brain which will cause her to have seizures for the rest of her life. She takes a lot of medicine, including Dilantin and phenobarbital. This requires someone to be with her around the clock. Are you sure you want to take on this responsibility?"

"I realize she is sick," I said. "But I love her; and more than anything, I want to marry her." And that is what we did on July 3, 1984. We were so young when we married we didn't know if we needed to go on a honeymoon or to summer camp.

After being married for only a short period of time, I began to realize just how sick Barbara really was. She had seizures frequently. She would have them at home, at church, even at the grocery store. It seemed like she had them everywhere. After paying for someone to stay with her while I was at work and for the expensive medication she was required to take as well as doctor bills, our finances were a mess. Our outgo was exceeding our income, and our upkeep was our downfall. At the end of the month, there would always be more month than money. It was obvious we were heading for financial disaster. I remember many Fridays receiving my check from the machine shop where I worked and praying I had enough gas to get to the bank to cash my check and then make it to the gas station. I had wired up and taped up my boots many times because I did not have the money to buy the shoes I needed. I worked many hours running an extremely hot milling machine in an unairconditioned shop and yet did not even have the money to buy a soft drink. I simply believed — and still do believe — that my wife's needs come first; therefore, we used our money to provide for her care and medicine.

I can still remember coming in from work one evening and

Barbara telling me she believed God had divinely touched her and healed her from having seizures. I am saddened to report that I did not get too excited. I guess I did not have the faith I should have had. I told her that was great but to keep taking her medicine.

Several days passed, and she said to me again: "I do not need the medicine. God has touched me." So I made a compromise with her. I said for her to take the medicine Monday through Friday. Then on Saturday and Sunday when I was home, she could go without it. She consented just to make me happy but made sure I knew again that God had touched her and there was no need for the medicine.

A few days passed. While I was running a vertical milling machine, I was talking to the Lord: "Lord, I cannot be with Barbara Monday through Friday. Lord, she must take her medicine." That is when God spoke to me: "Son, what can you do that I can't do? I am with her every day!" Someone asked me how I knew that was God. If He ever speaks to you, you will never have to ask me that again. Anyway, I became so emotional I had to ask my supervisor if I could go home. I ran to my car; and as fast as I could, I drove home. I walked in and told Barbara she did not ever have to take her medicine again. That was more than fifteen years ago, and she has not had one seizure! I learned early *there is no problem too big for Jesus to solve.*

The second thing I learned from this story is *there is no person too small for Jesus to use.* Jesus used a small lad's lunch to feed the multitude. There is no person too small for Jesus to use, but there are people too big for Jesus to use.

Hudson Taylor was asked why God used him to do such awesome mission work in China. He responded, "God looked until He found someone small enough to do the job." The Bible is very clear that God uses those people who are little in their own sight. Samuel said to King Saul, "When thou wast little in thine own sight, wast thou not made the head of the tribes of Israel, and the LORD anointed thee king over Israel?" (1 Samuel 15:17).

A story that well illustrates this point is the experience of missionary Milton Cunningham. Milton was flying from Atlanta to Dallas. When he found his seat, it happened to be the middle seat in the section. To his right next to the window was a young girl who obviously had Down syndrome. The young girl began asking him some very simple but almost offensive questions. "Mister, did you brush your teeth this morning?" she asked. He looked rather shocked at the question but responded, "Well, yes, I brushed my teeth this morning." The girl said, "Good. That's what you're supposed to do." Then she asked, "Mister, do you smoke?" Again Milton was a little uncomfortable but told her with a little chuckle that he did not. She said, "Good 'cause that will make you die." Then she said, "Mister, do you love Jesus?" Milton was really caught off guard by the simplicity and the forthrightness of her questions. He smiled and said, "Well, yes, I do love Jesus." The young girl with Down syndrome just smiled and said, "Good 'cause we're all supposed to love Jesus."

About the time the plane was getting ready for takeoff, another gentleman sat down beside Milton on the aisle seat. He began reading a magazine. The young girl nudged Milton and said, "Mister, ask him if he brushed his teeth this morning." Milton was really uneasy with that one and said he was not going to do it.

That girl continued to nudge Milton, saying: "Ask him! Ask him!" So Milton turned to the man seated next to him and said, "Sir, I don't mean to bother you; but my friend here wants me to ask you if you brushed your teeth this morning." The man looked startled, of course. But when he looked past Milton and saw the young girl sitting there, he could tell she had good intentions; so he took her question in stride and said with a smile: "Well, yes, I brushed my teeth this morning."

As the plane taxied down the runway and began to take off, the girl nudged Milton again and said, "Ask him if he smokes." And so Milton did. The man said the same thing Milton had said. As the plane lifted into the air, the young girl nudged Milton one last time and said, "Ask him if he loves Jesus." Milton turned to the fellow once more and said, "Now she wants to know if you love Jesus?" The man could have responded like he had to the previous questions — with a smile on his face and a chuckle in his voice; and he almost did. But then the smile on his face disappeared, and his expression became serious. He turned to Milton and said, "You know, honestly I can't say that I do. It's not that I don't want to; it's just that I don't know Him. I don't know how to know Him. I've wanted to be a person of faith all my life, but I haven't known how to do it. And now I've come to a time in my life when I really need that very much."

As the plane soared through the skies between Atlanta and as, Milton Cunningham listened to the man talk about his life was able to share his own personal story and testimony. He ared with the man how to become a person of faith. It all happened because God used a young girl with Down syndrome.

What does God want from you and me? The same thing He wanted from the lad: his lunch. The lunch represented everything he had. Notice three things about the lunch.

First of all, it was *transferred* to Jesus. The boy gave all of his lunch to the Lord. He did not say, "Jesus, You can have one of these fish and three loaves." He gave it all!

"Do you want to buy a cow?" asked a man. "Yes," answered the dairy farmer. "But what is her pedigree?" "What's that?" asked the man. "Forget it," said the farmer. "How much milk does she give?" "All she has," beamed the man.

Do you want to be used of God? Well, have you given everything to Him? He will be "Lord of all or not Lord at all."

Secondly, it was *taken* by Jesus. When you give Jesus something, He will receive it. Even if it is just a cup of cold water given in His name, He will receive it. There is no gift too small for Him to use.

Thirdly, it was *transformed* by Jesus. When Jesus took the ordinary loaves and fish and blessed them, they produced extraordinary results. It is amazing how Jesus always seemingly used the unlikely. He used childless Abraham to be the father of a nation. He used undisciplined Samson to be a judge. He used a shepherd boy named David to be king. He used stuttering Moses to be the leader of Israel. He used unstable Peter to be the rock of the Church. There is no person too small for Jesus to use.

The third thing I learned from this story is there is no hunger too deep for Jesus to satisfy. The miracle that day is significant not because He fed the multitude but because, through it, He taught us He can meet the deeper spiritual hunger of our hearts.

Notice two things about Christ. The very next day these people came back to see Jesus. Their desire was to meet, eat, and retreat. They hoped they had found a perpetual cafeteria, a "bread Messiah." But notice what Jesus said to them in John 6:27, "Labour not for the meat which perisheth, but for that meat which endureth unto everlasting life." He said, "You are seeking temporary things, but I am eternal. Believe on Me, and ye shall eat Spiritual Bread."

The second thing we notice is Jesus not only is Spiritual Bread but also is Satisfying Bread. Now we come to the message in the miracle. Here is why Jesus fed the multitude. Jesus said to them, "I am the bread of life: he that cometh to me shall never hunger; and he that believeth on me shall never thirst" (John 6:35). Jesus is Satisfying Bread for our souls. People are searching everywhere for satisfaction, but they never will find that satisfaction until they find it in Jesus Christ.

The first sixteen years of my life I spent searching for satisfaction. No matter what I did, there was always something missing. I thank God for the night Rev. Clayton Jones led me to faith in Christ. I found peace, contentment, and satisfaction. "For he satisfieth the longing soul, and filleth the hungry soul with goodness" (Psalm 107:9).

A man was giving his testimony at one of the Salvation Army open-air meetings. As he was testifying, a heckler in the crowd yelled, "Why don't you shut up and sit down? You're just dreaming!" Immediately, the heckler felt a tug on his coat. He looked down to see a little girl who said, "Sir, may I speak to you? That man who is talking up there is my daddy. He used to spend all the money he made on whiskey. My mother was very sad and would cry most of the time. Sometimes when Daddy would come home, he would hit my mother. I didn't have shoes or a nice dress to wear to school. But look at my shoes now. And see this pretty dress? My daddy bought these for me. See my mother over there? She's the one with the bright smile on her face. She's happy now. She sings even when she's doing the ironing!" Then the little girl said, "Mister, if my daddy is dreaming, please don't wake him up." I am grateful Jesus transforms lives, and there is no hunger too deep for Him to satisfy.

As you can probably tell by now, I love stories. One of my favorite sports stories is about one of America's greatest baseball players, Ty Cobb. He played in 3,033 games — more than any other major league player. He scored more runs (2,245 — until Rickey Henderson in 2001); made more hits (4,191— until Pete Rose in 1985); stole more bases (892); and finished with a higher lifetime batting average (.367) than any other major leaguer. He led the American League in batting twelve times — nine years in a row. Three times his batting average was over 400. But the Cobb record that baseball historians talked about most were the 96 bases he stole in 1915, a record finally broken by Lou Brock.

On July 17, 1961, a preacher came to visit Ty Cobb in the hospital. He told Cobb how to be born again. Cobb looked up from his deathbed and said, "You're telling me that a whole life of sin can be done away with by a deathbed repentance." The preacher said, "No, Mr. Cobb, I'm not telling you that a deathbed repentance can do away with a lifetime of sin. What I am telling you is that the blood of Jesus can." At that moment, Ty Cobb invited Jesus into his life. As the preacher was leaving his hospital room, Cobb said, "Tell all my friends that I am sorry I did this in the bottom of the ninth. If I had my life to do over, I would have done it in the top of the first." Jesus truly does satisfy.

CHAPTER FOUR

If You Want Your Pockets to Jingle, You Must Shake a Leg

Genesis 24:10-20

10. And the servant took ten camels of the camels of his master, and departed; for all the goods of his master were in his hand: and he arose, and went to Mesopotamia, unto the city of Nahor.

11. And he made his camels to kneel down without the city by a well of water at the time of the evening, even the time that women go out to draw water.

12. And he said, O LORD God of my master Abraham, I pray thee, send me good speed this day, and shew kindness unto my master Abraham.

13. Behold, I stand here by the well of water; and the daughters of the men of the city come out to draw water:

14. And let it come to pass, that the damsel to whom I shall say, Let down thy pitcher, I pray thee, that I may drink; and she shall say, Drink, and I will give thy

camels drink also: let the same be she that thou hast appointed for thy servant Isaac; and thereby shall I know that thou hast shewed kindness unto my master.

15. And it came to pass, before he had done speaking, that, behold, Rebekah came out, who was born to Bethuel, son of Milcah, the wife of Nahor, Abraham's brother, with her pitcher upon her shoulder.

16. And the damsel was very fair to look upon, a virgin, neither had any man known her: and she went down to the well, and filled her pitcher, and came up.

17. And the servant ran to meet her, and said, Let me, I pray thee, drink a little water of thy pitcher.

18. And she said, Drink, my lord: and she hasted, and let down her pitcher upon her hand, and gave him drink.

19. And when she had done giving him drink, she said, I will draw water for thy camels also, until they have done drinking.

20. And she hasted, and emptied her pitcher into the trough, and ran again unto the well to draw water, and drew for all his camels.

A man went to a local business seeking employment. The company's president stated to him: "I don't think we have enough work to keep you busy." The man responded, "You'd be surprised how little it takes."

Because a person is seeking employment does not necessarily mean they are seeking work. I recently read this announcement on an employee bulletin board: "In case of fire, flee the building with the same reckless abandonment that occurs each day at quitting time!"

Even though the work ethic seems to be at an all-time low, the Bible is very articulate that Christians should have a strong work ethic. The Bible teaches if a man is physically able to work and will not, the church is not to feed him but rather let him starve to death. ". . . that if any should not work, neither should he eat" (2 Thessalonians 3:10). That verse needs to be over the door of every welfare office in America. It is wrong to take money from a man who will work and give it to a man who won't! Work is a four-letter word America needs to learn.

President Theodore Roosevelt was right when he said, "Extend pity to no man because he has to work. If he is worth his salt, he will work. I envy the man who has work worth doing and does it well. Far and away, the best prize that life offers is the chance to work hard at work worth doing."

I recently read some alarming statistics. Did you know seventy percent of Americans do not like their jobs and twenty-nine percent equate their jobs to prison? It is vitally important that you like your job for many reasons; but can you believe it is the number one factor contributing to a long life? That's right; stats tell us the number one secret to a long life is not diet and exercise or one's family genes but occupational happiness. It is extremely imperative that we love our job; and when we do, we never have to go to work again! Allow me to share with you seven steps to occupational happiness.

The first step is to *play.* Proverbs 23:4 says, "Labor not to be rich" or to paraphrase: "Don't work just for the money." The secret to occupational happiness is to find something you enjoy doing and learn to do it well enough that others will pay you for doing it. If you hate your job, work toward quitting. Life is too

35

short to be that miserable. Now, if you have tried twelve jobs and you despised them all, then the problem is probably not the job - but the problem is you.

The second step to occupational happiness is to *go out of your way.* Allow me to give you some background to Genesis 24. Sarah, the wife of Abraham, had just died at the age of 127 years. Abraham also was well stricken in age. They had a son Isaac who was around thirty years of age; and in Old Testament times, it was the father's responsibility to choose a mate for his child. (As the father of a daughter, I wish we would go back to those principles.) Abraham and his son Isaac lived in Canaan, and Abraham knew the girls of Canaan worshipped only pagan gods. He could not bear the thought of his son marrying a girl who worshipped false gods. The Bible teaches a believer should not marry an unbeliever (2 Corinthians 6:14). When a Christian marries a nonChristian mate, they are unequally yoked. The Christian immediately gets the devil for a father-in-law!

Abraham then went to his eldest servant and said, "I want you to take ten camels loaded with goods and travel to the land of Mesopotamia and bring back a wife for my son." Apparently, Abraham's health forbade him from making the trip; therefore, he sent his most trusted servant.

Once the servant arrived in Mesopotamia, he made his camels kneel down to be watered and he made an unusual request of the Lord. He said, "Lord, please show kindness to my master Abraham and show me the wife for Isaac. Allow a damsel to come and offer me a drink and then offer water for my ten camels."

It came to pass — before he was done speaking — that behold a woman named Rebekah came to his side. She was a virgin who was very beautiful. She came to the servant and said, "Can I give you a drink?" And when she had finished giving him a drink, she started drawing water from the well for the camels. Now please understand this was a great task because a camel would drink from twenty to thirty gallons of water. This meant she possibly drew 300 gallons of water. Rebekah was willing to *go out of her way.*

Most people's work philosophy is to do the least amount expected and to get the most payment for it. But the Bible teaches that Christians are to go the extra mile and do more than is expected. I am convinced if Christians would go the extra mile one of the questions on job applications would be: "Are you a Christian?" The world would be beating church doors down seeking employees. Instead, many are like the man who went to the welfare office seeking assistance because he said he was having trouble with his eyes. The office worker said his application showed he had 20/20 vision. He told her that was right, but the problem was he couldn't see himself working. The truth is: "Nothing will work in your life until you do." My mother was correct when she said, "If you are going to rise to the top, you must first get off your bottom." God gave us a head to think with and a tail to sit on. Heads we win and tails we lose. Get to work!

The third step to occupational happiness is to *remember to pray.* Realize your job is more than a task; it is a ministry. Do you know the word *vocation* comes from the Latin word *vocare* which means "a call"? God wants your job to be a calling. Pastors and missionaries are not the only ones who are called. God has a special calling for each of us. Make sure you pray and find out what God's calling is for your life.

The fourth step to occupational happiness is to *be positive every day.* Happiness is not a position in the company but rather a disposition in the mind.

Hall of Fame player Stan Musial was known as one of baseball's most consistent players. One day, when Musial was playing for the St. Louis Cardinals, a teammate came into the clubhouse whistling. He turned to Musial and said, "I feel like I'm in a groove. I feel like I'm going to get two hits today! Ever feel like that Stan?" Smiling, Musial looked at him and said, "Every day!"

I encourage people to tell themselves the good things about their job. You may have flexible hours, paid sick days, a company car, an expense account, or a great boss. Be sure to remind yourself of those things. Welsh doctor turned preacher Martyn Lloyd-Jones asserted, "Most unhappiness in life is due to the fact that we are listening to ourselves rather than talking to ourselves."

The fifth step to occupational happiness is to *be careful what you say.* SUCCESS magazine tells us that eighty-seven percent of the people who are terminated are not let go because of their being incapable but because of their inability to get along with others. Frogs have the advantage over us because they can eat whatever bugs them. We can't. We must learn to work with other people — even though that sometimes may be difficult.

My greatest asset in learning how to get along with others happened a few years ago when I began to study personality profiles.

There are four basic personality types. You may not be 100 percent one type, but you will be a strong mixture of one or two. When you understand personalities, you begin to understand why people act and react in a certain way. Please understand there is no one profile better than the other. All personalities have strengths and weaknesses. Look at the four personality types below:

Choleric:
Paul was a choleric. Cholerics are usually leaders. They are the boss or at least they think they are. They are opinionated and love a challenge. They do have strengths. They can fix a problem; they are strong willed; they have confidence; and they think the only reason Rome was not built in a day was because they weren't captain of the crew. They are "doers." (I think I know a choleric!) They also have weaknesses. They are bossy; they can't relax; they have a tendency to make others feel less than; and they are sometimes workaholics.

Sanguine:
Peter was a sanguine. Sanguines love to talk, love to party, love to laugh, and love to dress in loud colors. They also have strengths. They love people, have a good sense of humor, are usually popular, and are very creative. They also have weaknesses. They can't say no, are unorganized (Tarzan would get hurt walking through their bedroom), don't follow through, and talk so much that they don't listen.

Melancholy:
Thomas was a melancholy. Melancholies see the dark side of everything. They are perfectionists; every hair is in place. They iron their

underwear and actually read the instructions before putting some-thing together. They have strengths. They are neat, work well alone, are persistent, and usually are great with numbers. They also have weaknesses. They are negative, have selective hearing, are unforgiving, and are very suspicious of others. There is not much difference in hugging an ironing board and hugging a melancholy.

Phlegmatic:
Tabitha was a phlegmatic. They are easygoing, cool, calm and col-lected, peaceful. Their strengths are patience, quietness, noncon-frontational, and are congenial. Their weaknesses are that they can be lazy, hard to get moving, stubborn, unenthusiastic, and not a risk taker.

I trust this brief synopsis of temperaments will enable you to better understand yourself and the people with whom you work.

The sixth step to occupational happiness is to *prepare to pay.* "Everything nice has a price" and "There is no free lunch" are phrases related to this slogan.

Every day Rebekah went to this very same well to draw water for her family. A trivial, small job one might say; but because she did not despise the small job, she became the wife of one of the greatest men in the Bible. And, too, she was blessed to be in the direct line of ancestresses of the Lord Jesus Christ.

David did not start out as King of Israel. He started out as a shepherd to a small herd of sheep. General Colin Powell did not start out as Secretary of State. He started out mopping floors in a soft drink plant. Do not despise the small job. Everything nice has a price!

The last step to occupational happiness is to *plan to stay*. Once you have decided what you are destined to do and you enjoy it, plan to stay. You cannot change jobs and fields every year and expect to be successful. Did you know that in the largest ten churches in America the average tenure of the pastor is twenty-four years?

Dave Thomas, founder of Wendy's, said, "Only do one thing at a time and only a few things in a lifetime."

My dear friend, Bill Purvis, gives a wonderful illustration. He says, "A mushroom will grow in six hours, but you really don't have anything. Plus you can kick it over very easily. But an oak tree takes sixty years to grow; and with those massive roots and huge limbs, you are not going to just kick it over. You have something." I decided I wanted to be an oak tree. I can be one because an oak tree is just a nut that refused to quit. I plan to stay!

If you want your pockets to jingle, you must shake a leg. Let me give employers some things they can do to help their employees "shake a leg."

1. *Give proper training.* One employer said, "If I train my people, I will lose them." There is something worse than training people and losing them. It is not training them and keeping them.
2. *Explain your expectations.* Employees want and need a clear job description.
3. *Settle the salary.* When an employer hires someone and tells him he can pay between $500 and $600 a week, the employer hears $500 while the employee hears the figure

$600. An understanding avoids a misunderstanding. Settle the salary.

4. *Be honest!* Do what you say you are going to do — no matter what.

5. *Give recognition.* People need continual affirmation, so they know they are meeting a need and doing it well.

6. *Be loyal.* Ronald Reagan's White House Chief of Staff Donald Regan said, "You've got to give loyalty down if you want loyalty up." Be loyal to your people.

7. *Give financial increases.* All people respond to praises and raises. If you want good employees, pay good money. If you pay peanuts, you will get monkeys.

8. *Assign their favorite work.* Reward good work by assigning people tasks they enjoy doing.

9. *Trust.* If you believed in an employee enough to hire him, trust him enough to do his job.

10. *Offer personal advancement opportunities.* People who produce should be given the opportunity to advance.

Herb Kelleher, founder of Southwest Airlines, understands these principles. On Boss's Day in 1994, a full-page ad appeared in *USA Today.* It was contracted and paid for by the employees of the airline. It said:

THANKS, HERB

For remembering every one of our names,

For supporting the Ronald McDonald House,

For helping load baggage on Thanksgiving,

For giving everyone a kiss (and we mean everyone),

For listening,

For running the only profitable major airline,

For singing at our holiday party,

For singing only once a year,

For letting us wear shorts and sneakers to work,

For golfing at the LUV Classic with only one club,

For out talking Sam Donaldson,

For riding your Harley Davidson into Southwest
Headquarters,

For being a friend, not just a boss.

Happy Boss's Day from each one of your 16,000 employees!

CHAPTER FIVE

There Is No Other Place Anywhere Near This Place Like This Place; This Must Be the Place

Acts 11:19-30 / Acts 13:1-3

19. Now they which were scattered abroad upon the persecution that arose about Stephen travelled as far as Phenice, and Cyprus, and Antioch, preaching the word to none but unto the Jews only.

20. And some of them were men of Cyprus and Cyrene, which, when they were come to Antioch, spake unto the Grecians, preaching the Lord Jesus.

21. And the hand of the Lord was with them: and a great number believed, and turned unto the Lord.

22. Then tidings of these things came unto the ears of the church which was in Jerusalem: and they sent forth Barnabas, that he should go as far as Antioch.

23. Who, when he came, and had seen the grace of God, was glad, and exhorted them all, that with purpose of heart they would cleave unto the Lord.

24. For he was a good man, and full of the Holy Ghost

and of faith: and much people was added unto the
Lord.

25. Then departed Barnabas to Tarsus, for to seek Saul:

26. And when he had found him, he brought him unto
    Antioch. And it came to pass, that a whole year they
    assembled themselves with the church, and taught
    much people. And the disciples were called
    Christians first in Antioch.

27. And in these days came prophets from Jerusalem
    unto Antioch.

28. And there stood up one of them named Agabus, and
    signified by the spirit that there should be great
    dearth throughout all the world: which came to pass
    in the days of Claudius Caesar.

29. Then the disciples, every man according to his abili-
    ty, determined to send relief unto the brethren which
    dwelt in Judea:

30. Which also they did, and sent it to the elders by the
    hands of Barnabas and Saul.

Chapter 13

1. Now there were in the church that was at Antioch
   certain prophets and teachers; as Barnabas, and
   Simeon that was called Niger, and Lucius of Cyrene,
   and Manaen, which had been brought up with
   Herod the tetrarch, and Saul.

2. As they ministered to the Lord, and fasted, the Holy
   Ghost said, Separate me Barnabas and Saul for the
   work whereunto I have called them.

3. And when they had fasted and prayed, and laid their
   hands on them, they sent them away.

If there were a place in the New Testament like no other place anywhere near that place, that place would have been Antioch. I love to study churches and have had the privilege of visiting some of the greatest ones in our world. But I believe, if there was a model church, it was the church of Antioch situated three hundred miles north of Jerusalem.

Antioch had some wonderful qualities, but what is so amazing is that we can incorporate each of these qualities into our local fellowship and make our church "the place like no other place." Notice the seven qualities the church at Antioch possessed.

First, they had *the supernatural power of God.* The Bible says, ". . . the hand of the Lord was with them" (Acts 11:21). All of our promotions, programs, personalities, and plans will not replace the power of God. Most churches are beginning at eleven o'clock sharp and ending at twelve o'clock dull. They simply need God's power!

A pastor was leading a small, rural, declining church. The church was so far back in the sticks that the zip code was e-i-e-i-o. This pastor was so discouraged. He heard about a thriving, growing church in the city several miles away and decided to visit. He was hoping to hear something encouraging that would ignite his church.

Once he arrived and was seated in this plush, modern auditorium, he saw the pastor in his ceremonial robe walking down the aisle. He was carrying a golden pot with incense burning, repeating, "Holy, Holy, Holy." The rural pastor thought: *That's it! That's just what we need!* He immediately went back to his church board, seeking their approval. They were somewhat apprehensive about this idea and gave many reasons not to approve it — one being they had no golden pots. "We're just a poor, rural church," they said. The pastor responded, "I've" thought about that and know what we can do. We can get Folgers coffee cans and put moss in the bottom, and there will always be a deacon or two in the service with a cigarette lighter we can use to light our pots." He planned that the next Sunday he would stand in the pulpit and say, "Bring forth the incense pots"; and the men would walk down the aisle with the moss burning. This would be an awesome service!

Sunday came; and while the pastor was standing in the pulpit, he said, "Bring forth the incense pots." Nothing happened. He wondered if the men in the foyer could not hear him, so he shouted louder: "Bring forth the incense pots!" Again, nothing happened. The third time he yelled, "Bring forth the incense pots!" This time a voice spoke back: "We ain't got no incense pots. We threw them out the window 'cause the bottoms got hot!"

Churches are trying everything to replace God's power and presence, but there is no substitute. The text tells us the headquarters for the Christian Church at this time was the city of Jerusalem. They sent Barnabas to visit the church at Antioch. (Acts 11:22) We learn that when he arrived he saw the grace of God. For many years, I wondered, "How is the grace of God seen?" I know what it is like to experience the grace of God but had never seen it. Then I realized he saw Jews and Greeks worshipping God together. (Acts 11:19-20) These people had a history of hating each other, but the grace and power of God removed that barrier. We have many barriers in our churches today, and I am convinced only the supernatural power of God can break these strongholds.

We must realize God's supernatural power is for today as well. "Jesus Christ the same yesterday, and to day, and for ever" (Hebrews 13:8). We have no problem with the yesterday. We believe the ark survived the water; Moses parted the water; the ax head floated on the water; and Jesus walked on the water. We also have no problem with the forever. We believe that Jesus is coming back to rapture us home; we will meet Him in the sky and will forever be with Him. The trumpet will toot, and we will scoot. Not an airplane flight but a plain air flight. We will leave like Superman and come back like the Lone Ranger! My black preacher friend says, "I will stand before my Boss, take my loss, eat my supper, and come back on my hoss." We have no problem with forever.

Our problem is lack of belief in God's supernatural power for today. Can He restore my marriage, heal me of cancer, save my wayward child, or resurrect our lifeless church? The answer is *yes!* God is a great God who can "do exceeding, abundantly above all that we ask or think" (Ephesians 3:20); but we must desire His supernatural power.

The second quality that the church had was *they were serious about prayer and fasting.* The church at Antioch gave much time to prayer and fasting. (Acts 13:2-3) Any church that makes a difference for God must place great priority in these two areas.

John Wesley was correct when he stated, "God does nothing but by prayer everything with it." I am convinced the church of today is spending too much time feasting in the supper room and not enough time fasting in the upper room.

Do you know the largest Methodist, Presbyterian, and

Assemblies of God churches in our world are in Korea? Do you know the average Korean pastor prays for two hours a day? What about the amount of time spent in prayer by the average pastor in America? The answer is eight to nine minutes a day. If the devil can't make us bad, he will make us busy. Before Pentecost, the early church prayed ten days and preached ten minutes; they saw three thousand saved. We are preaching ten days, praying ten minutes, and seeing few saved. We must return to the altar of prayer!

2 Chronicles 7:14 says, "If my people, which are called by my name, shall humble themselves, and pray, and seek my face, and turn from their wicked ways; then will I hear from heaven, and will forgive their sin, and will heal their land."

There was a small town that had two churches and one whiskey distillery. Members of both churches complained the distillery gave the community a bad image. To make matters worse, the owner of the distillery was an atheist. The church members had tried unsuccessfully for two years to shut down the distillery. Finally, they decided to hold a Saturday night group prayer meeting and ask God to intervene and settle this once and for all. Saturday night came, and the church folks gathered together. During the entire meeting, a terrible electrical storm raged. To the delight of the church members, lightning struck the distillery and it burned to the ground.

The next morning the sermon in both churches was on the power of prayer. The insurance adjusters promptly notified the distillery owner they would not pay for the damages since it was caused by an act of God. They told him "acts of God" were excluded from his policy. The owner was infuriated and decided to sue the churches, claiming they had conspired with God to destroy his building and business. The church members emphatically denied having anything to do with the cause of the incident. The judge hearing the case opened the trial with these words: "I find one thing about this case most perplexing. We have a situation here where the plaintiff, an atheist, is professing his belief in the power of prayer and the defendants, the church members, are denying that very same power."

The third quality was *strong leadership.* Notice Barnabas saw a need for leadership and went to Tarsus to bring Paul back to help provide it. (Acts 11:22-26) Everything rises and falls on leadership. Churches, businesses, or any other type of organization will never grow around their leader; they grow under a leader. To grow a club, church, or organization, you must first grow its leader. If an organization is growing, they have a strong leader. If an organization is not growing, it has a leadership problem.

This humorous story underscores the importance of effective leadership. During a sales meeting, the manager was berating the sales staff for their dismally low sales figures. "I've had just about enough of poor performance and excuses," he said. "If you can't do the job, perhaps there are other people out there who would jump at the chance to sell the worthy products each of you have the privilege to represent." Then pointing to a newly recruited, retired pro-football player, he said, "If a football team isn't winning, what happens? The players are replaced, right?" The question hung heavy for a few seconds; then the ex-football player answered, "Actually, sir, if the whole team was having trouble, we usually got a new coach."

With the fact established that leadership is vitally important, what is leadership? Leadership is influence. That is it; nothing more, nothing less. I love the Chinese Leadership Proverb that says, "He who thinketh he leadeth and hath no one following him is only taking a walk." The real leaders in any organization are not the ones with positions and titles but the ones with followers. Below are ten steps to increasing influence.

1. **Character:** Be in reality what you appear to be.
2. **Competence:** You don't teach what you don't know and you don't lead where you don't go. Skill is important!
3. **Develop a passion for people:** John Maxwell was correct when he said, "People don't care how much you know until they know how much you care."
4. **Always accept your share of the blame.**
5. **Share the credit when things go well.**
6. **Smile a lot and have a positive attitude.**
7. **Be an encourager.**
8. **Learn names of people.**
9. **Learn to say, "I'm sorry."**
10. **Learn to read people correctly.**

The fourth quality the church at Antioch possessed was they were *steadfast in discipleship.* They taught the people a full year even before they were called Christians. In the average church today, we are satisfied if people just show up. God wants us to do more than show up; He wants us to grow up. That only comes through discipleship. The responsibility of the church is threefold:

1. Make them by winning them to Christ.
2. Mark them by baptizing them.
3. Mature them by discipling.

John 4:24 says, "God is a Spirit: and they that worship him must worship him in spirit and in truth." We have a group of people today who place all of the emphasis on Spirit-filled worship. They equate worship with how much emotion is expressed in a service. But I know you can't tell how much gas is in a tank by the honk of the horn. These people will eventually blow up!

Then there is another group who place all of the emphasis on truth. They enjoy the deep things of God. They enjoy studying transubstantiation, consubstantiation, and an expositional study of the laws of Leviticus. They are answering questions no one is asking. I heard about a man who physically died in such a church. When the paramedics came, they carried out twenty-five men before they got the right one! A group like this will dry up.

God wants us to have a balance: "spirit and truth." He wants us to worship Him in a spiritual environment and have solid teachings and preaching from the Word of God. We then will not blow up or dry up but grow up. The church at Antioch was steadfast in their discipleship.

The fifth quality the church at Antioch had was *a spirit of generosity.* There was a famine throughout the entire Roman Empire, and the church at Antioch sent relief to their brethren who lived in Judea. (Acts 11:29) There will come a time in the life of any church when the generosity of the people will be tested.

One creative pastor was determined to have a record-breaking missions offering. He wired his pews with electrical currents and placed a buzzer on the pulpit. On Sunday, at offering time, he asked, "How many will stand and pledge $100 to the world missions offering?" He then pressed the buzzer, giving everyone an electrical shock! Dozens stood immediately! He reported that his congregation gave a record-breaking offering; but to his dismay, several deacons were electrocuted! When it comes to giving, some people stop at nothing.

The sixth quality the church at Antioch possessed was *a sense of vision.* This church sent Paul and Barnabas on their first missionary journey. Yes, before the printing press, automobile, TV, or satellite, they had a vision for the world. The Bible says, "Where there is no vision, the people perish . . ." (Proverbs 29:18).

Helen Keller was asked, "What would be worse than being born blind?" She replied, "To have sight but without vision." Sad as it is, we have scores of people in leadership positions with no vision for their organizations. A pastor was continually praying, "God give me power. God give me power." Eventually, the Lord spoke to him and said, "With a vision no bigger than you have, you don't need My power."

I cannot express emphatically enough the importance of vision to the future of any organization. You must see it and say it before you will seize it. When Walt Disney World first opened, Mrs. Disney was asked to speak at the Grand Opening. Since Walt had died, she was introduced; and the emcee said, "Mrs. Disney, I just wish Walt could have seen this." She stood up and said, "He did," and sat down. Vision is vital!

The seventh quality possessed by the church at Antioch was *soul winning as a passion.* The Bible tells us "a great number believed" (Acts 11:21). Did you know that not one time in the entire Word of God does the Bible tell an unsaved person to go to church? Granted, many times He commands the child of God to go but never a nonChristian. He commands the children of God to go into the highways and hedges and bring them in. As far as the house of God is concerned, we are to attend it, extend it, and defend it. We need to get off our seat, onto our feet, and into the street, sharing Jesus with men, women, boys, and girls. We ought to be just nobodies that are telling everybody about Somebody who can change anybody.

I do have a passion for souls. However, it saddens me to report my passion because it came out of great pain. Many times our passion is a result of our pain.

I was pastoring a church in Tennessee, and the church seemed to be doing well. The church was growing; the finances were good; and I was well liked. It hurts me to admit that in my early ministry I was more interested in pleasing people than in being respected by people.

We had a lady in our community go into Winchester Hospital, and I was pretty certain she was not a Christian. I made several visits to see her, but I never shared Christ with her. One Saturday evening, I was visiting near the hospital and God spoke to my heart to go and see her. I said to God and to myself that I would be in the area again on Monday and I would just go then.

The very next morning, I got up and went to r̃
still see the man pulling me off to the side ⸴̃
you hear what happened last night?" My h̀
shared the news of the death of the woma̱

nights, I could not sleep. I constantly saw her in my dreams. It breaks my heart even now; and I cry as I write, thinking if that lady did not get saved, her blood will be on my hands at the Judgment Seat of Christ. (Ezekiel 3:18) I promised it would never happen again. I made a commitment I would always share Christ.

Just a few days later, God gave me the opportunity to go to Saint Thomas Hospital in Nashville, Tennessee, to visit a twenty-three-year-old girl who needed heart and lung transplants. I arrived at 7 p.m. and told the young lady God's plan of salvation. It was a wonderful experience to see her remove the oxygen mask and pray the sinner's prayer with me. I can still hear her say, "The guilt and condemnation is gone, and I feel so clean." I left the hospital around 8 p.m. and received a call around midnight that she had died. I will never forget how I felt over the fact that she had received Christ, but I couldn't help remembering the lady in Winchester. I kept thinking I might have led her to Christ just that easily if I had shared Him with her. I do have a passion for souls, but it comes out of great pain.

Determine to incorporate these seven qualities into your church. If you do, I promise there will be no other place anywhere near your place like your place; and your place will be the place!

CHAPTER SIX

The Frog Said, 'Time Is Fun When You Are Having Flies'

TIME MANAGEMENT

Ben Franklin said, "Dost thou love life? Then do not squander time; for that's the stuff life is made of." The Bible says, "See then that ye walk circumspectly, not as fools, but as wise. Redeeming the time, because the days are evil" (Ephesians 5:15-16). To paraphrase: "Be careful the way you live your life; for you can either live a wise or foolish lifestyle." The wise lifestyle uses one's minutes, hours, days, and years wisely; and the foolish lifestyle uses them unwisely.

A teacher, instructing his class on the subject of time ma̶ ment, illustrated with a powerful object lesson. He t̶ glass jar and put some large rocks in it and then ̶ the jar was full. The class responded, "Yes." ̶ gravel into the jar and asked again if t̶ "Yes." He then poured water into ̶ tion, and they responded wi̶

"Class, what is the meaning of this time-management illustration?" A student in the back of the class raised his hand and stated, "No matter how busy you are, you can do more." The teacher said he was incorrect. The message is: "You better put the big things in your life first, or you will never get them in."

Every individual must do a personal evaluation to decide what the big things are in his or her life. For me, it is simple. It is my faith, my family, my friends, and my freedom. Those are my big things; and I must put them in the jar first, or I may not get them in.

I want you to notice five characteristics of time.

First, is the *value of time.* Time is valuable. To constantly remind me of this, I keep a small card in my wallet and try to read it every day. It reads, "This is the beginning of a new day. God has given me this day to use as I will. I can waste it or use it for good, but what I do today is important because I am exchanging a day of my life for it! When tomorrow comes, this day will be gone forever, leaving in its place something I have traded for it. I want it to be gain and not loss, good and not evil, success and not failure in order that I shall not regret the price that I have paid for it."

The Bible commands us to redeem the time in Ephesians 5. To redeem is to rescue from going to waste. Time is the passing of life. Simply put, if we don't manage our time, we are wasting our lives. Probably nothing better illustrates the value of time than the statement Queen Elizabeth I made on her deathbed: "I would give my entire kingdom for one more moment." Time is valuable!

Secondly, I want you to see the *vanishing of time.* For what is your life? "It is even a vapour, that appeareth for a little time, and then vanisheth away" (James 4:14). Time certainly does move extremely fast; either you use it or lose it because it waits for no one.

I love to tell the story about the man who went to the doctor; and after having a variety of tests, he was told he had only one year to live. He then asked the doctor if he had any advice. The doctor said, "Yes, there is a lady that lives out on the south end of the county. She is not attractive, and she lives in a small four-room house with no plumbing or electricity. She has ten children, and the oldest is twelve. I suggest you marry her." The man asked if that would make him live longer. The doctor replied, "No, but it will be the longest year you've ever lived." Time is vanishing!

Thirdly, I want you to notice the *violators of our time.* The question is not: "Is your calendar full?" The question is: "What has filled your calendar?" Only you can determine that. I am convinced there are three primary violators of our time.

1. *Misplaced Priorities:*

What are the priorities and goals you have for your life? Have you written them down? Are you doing the things that reflect your priorities? Hypothetically, if your priority is to develop a close walk with God, does your schedule include ample time for prayer, meditation, and Bible study? You cannot get closer to God without taking time for these things. Several people spend hours on the phone each day in what I call "idle chatter": "How are you doing?" "Fine." "What have you been up to?" "Nothing much." They have no reason for calling, yet they spend hours on the phone. Simply stated, "Have a reason for what you do!"

2. *Procrastination:*

Procrastinators have great plans, ideas, and solutions. The only problem is they never get around to them. Their favorite word is "tomorrow"; and at the end of their lives, they have only lots of empty yesterdays.

3. *Lack of Concentration:*

I realize we live during a time in which you hear much talk about multi-tasking. But I am convinced successful people focus on one project and complete it. The Apostle Paul said, ". . . this one thing I do . . . " (Philippians 3:13). Orville Redenbacher said, "Only do one thing, and do it uncommonly well."

Experienced animal trainers take a stool with them when they step into a cage with a lion. Why a stool? It tames a lion better than anything. When the trainer holds the stool with the legs extended towards the lion's face, the animal tries to focus on all four legs at once, therefore paralyzing him. Divided focus always works against you and thwarts efficiency.

Fourth is the *victory of our time.* Below are eight keys to good time management.

1. *Assume Responsibility:*

You are responsible for managing your own time. Henry Ford was famous for dropping into his employees' offices. When he was asked why he did that, he simply replied, "I can leave the other fellow's office quicker than I can get him to leave mine." Assume responsibility for managing your time.

2. *Seek God's Guidance:*

The Bible says, "As we have therefore opportunity, let us do good unto all men . . ." (Galatians 6:10). The word for *opportunity* in the Greek is "making the most of your time." Ask God to provide opportunities for you to use your time, talents, and treasures wisely.

3. *Learn How to Wake Up and Get Up:*

"How long wilt thou sleep, O sluggard? when wilt thou arise out of thy sleep? Yet a little sleep, a little slumber, a little folding of the hands to sleep" (Proverbs 6:9-10). I call this principle: "The Mind over Mattress Principle." What if I told you I could get you two additional weeks of vacation every year? Now that would be worth the price of this book, wouldn't it? Here's how I can. All you have to do is get up fifteen minutes earlier each morning. Learn how to wake up and get up!

4. *Plan Your Schedule:*

Each week I have a three-fold priority list. First are the things I must do: to provide leadership to the staff, to prepare by prayer and study, and to meet/counsel/conference with individuals. Secondly, I have things I should do: to visit a hospital or a new family in the community. Thirdly, I have things that would be nice to do: send someone a card, give someone a call, buy someone a gift, or take someone out to dinner.

In the 1930s, Charles Schwab, president of the Bethlehem Steel Corp., was really struggling with time management in his company. He simply felt he, his managers, and his workers were not managing their time effectively. He hired Ivey Lee to assist him with this problem. Mr. Lee instructed them to write down on a blank piece of paper each morning the things they needed to accomplish that day in the order of their importance. Mr. Schwab asked what he owed for this advice. Mr. Lee answered, "Try it; and if it works for you, pay me what you think it's worth." Two months later, Charles Schwab sent Ivey Lee a check for $25,000. Keep in mind that was the 1930s. Plan your schedule!

5. *Stay Organized:*

"Let all things be done decently and in order" (1 Corinthians 14:40). I am convinced Jesus was very organized. After He was resurrected from the tomb and Peter came, the Bible says, "And the napkin, that was about his head, not lying with the linen clothes, but wrapped together in a place by itself" (John 20:7). Jesus took the time to fold the napkin that was wrapped around His head even during His resurrection. How did you leave your bed this morning?

Did you know executives spend six weeks a year looking for files, phone numbers, and other lost or misplaced items? Get organized! Don't be like the lady that said, "I write everything down that I want to remember. That way, instead of spending a lot of time trying to remember what it was I wrote down, I spend the time looking for the paper I wrote it on."

6. *Learn to Delegate:*

"If one put a thousand to flight, two can put ten thousand to flight" (Deuteronomy 32:30). It was a great day in my life and ministry when I quit trying to be the Lone Ranger (even he had Tonto). You lose hours because you do not delegate effectively on the job. If delegation is so helpful, why don't we do it? Here are two reasons. First, we desire job security. A weak leader worries that, if he helps subordinates, he will become dispensable. Actually, the opposite is true. The only way to make yourself indispensable is to make yourself dispensable by delegating to others and empowering them. In turn, you become so valuable to the organization that you are indispensable. The second reason is self-worth. Many people gain their value as a person from their work or position. We should get our self-worth from who we are in Christ and not who we are in the company.

7. *Eliminate the Unimportant:*

Most people waste time the same way every day. I have known people who spend hours opening their mail. Did you know eighty-four percent of mail is junk? I open my mail the same way every day at the same place, and that is over the trash can. It helps to avoid a messy desk. Another waste of my time is a pointless meeting — meetings that simply do not accomplish anything in which we take minutes and waste hours.

8. *Review Your Day:*

Ask yourself four questions at the end of every day:
   1. Did I make good use of my time?
   2. Did I procrastinate?
   3. Did I maintain my concentration?
   4. Did I make progress toward the accomplishment of my God-given goals?

Hopefully, most of your days, you will be able to answer yes to the questions; but I assure you there will be days when you will not. Simply; ask God to forgive you, and put the principles into action the next morning.

Lastly are the **vitals of our time.** There are three things that are vital for each and every one of us to do.

1. *Receive Christ as Your Personal Savior:*

Luke 16 tells us about a rich man who died and went to Hell and about a beggar who died and went to Abraham's bosom. The rich man cried and said, "Father Abraham, have mercy on me, and send Lazarus, that he may dip the tip of his finger in water, and cool my tongue, for I am tormented in this flame" (Luke16:24). But Abraham said, "Son, remember . . . in thy lifetime. . . ." Notice "lifetime" in Luke 16:25. There is no second chance! We must receive Christ during our lifetime, or it is too late. Eternity is too long to be wrong. A vital for everyone is receiving Christ as his or her personal Savior!

2. *Find Your God-Given Gifts and Use Them:*

"As every man hath received the gift, even so minister the same one to another, as good stewards of the manifold grace of God" (1 Peter 4:10). We all are gifted children of God, and we simply must find what we are destined to do and do it.

A thirty-eight-year-old scrubwoman would go to the movies and sigh: "If I only had her looks." She would listen to a singer and moan: "If I only had a voice like that." Then one day, someone gave her a copy of the book *The Magic of Believing.* She stopped comparing herself with the actresses and the singers. She stopped crying about what she did not have and started concentrating on what she did have. She took inventory of herself and remembered that in high school she had a reputation for being the funniest girl around. She began to turn her liabilities into assets. Phyllis Diller made millions because of her ability to make people laugh. She was not good looking, and she had a scratchy voice; but she could make people laugh. Find your God-given gifts and use them!

3. *Realize What Is Really Important:*

I agree with my mentor John Maxwell when he says, "Real success is the love and respect of those closest to us." Something is wrong when those who know you the least respect you the most. I want my radio listeners, congregation, community, and colleagues to respect me. But more than any of them, I want my precious wife Barbara and daughter Savannah Abigail to respect me because they are the most important people on Earth to me. I think the story of "A Thousand Marbles" will explain my point.

The older I get, the more I enjoy Saturday mornings. Perhaps it is the quiet solitude that comes with being the first one to rise, or maybe it is the unbounded joy of not having to be at work. Either way, the first few hours of a Saturday morning are the most enjoyable.

A few weeks ago, I was shuffling toward the kitchen with a cup of coffee in one hand and the morning paper in the other. What began as a typical Saturday morning turned into one of those lessons that the Lord hands you from time to time. I turned the volume up on my radio to listen to a Saturday morning talk show. I heard an older sounding man with a golden voice. He was talking about a thousand marbles to a man named Tom. I was intrigued and sat down to listen. He said, "Well, Tom, it sure seems like you are busy with your job. I'm sure they pay you well, but it's a shame you have to be away from your home and your family so much. Hard to believe a young fellow should have to work sixty or seventy hours a week to make ends meet. Too bad you missed your daughter's dance recital." He continued, "Let me tell you something, Tom — something that has helped me keep a good perspective on my priorities." This is when he began to explain his theory of a thousand marbles.

He began: "I sat down one day and did a little arithmetic. The average person lives about seventy-five years. I know some live more; some live less; but on average, folks live about this long. Now I multiplied 75 times 52 and came up with 3900 which is the number of Saturdays that an average person would have in his life-time. Now stick with me, Tom. I'm getting to the important part. It took me until I was fifty-five years old to think about all of this in any detail; and by that time, I had lived more than 2800 Saturdays. I got to thinking that if I lived to be seventy-five, I only had about 1000 Saturdays left to enjoy.

"So I went to a toy store and bought every single marble they had. I ended up having to visit three stores to round up 1000 marbles. I took them home and put them inside a large container next to the radio right here in my workshop. Every Saturday since then, I have taken one marble out and thrown it away. I found that by watching the marbles diminish, I focused more on the really important things in my life. There is nothing like watching your time here on this earth run out to get your priorities straight.

"Now let me tell you one last thing before I sign off with you and take my lovely wife to breakfast. This morning I took the very last marble out of the container. I figure, if I make it until next Saturday, then I will have been given a little extra time. It was nice to talk with you, Tom. I hope you spend more time with your loved ones, and I hope to meet you again someday. Have a good morning."

You could have heard a pin drop when he finished. Even the show's moderator did not have anything to say for a few moments. Then he began to say, "I guess he gave us all a lot to think about. I had planned to do some work that morning and then go to the gym. Instead I went upstairs and woke my wife with a kiss and said for her to c'mon because I was taking her and the kids out to breakfast. 'What brought this on?' she asked with a smile. I told her nothing special. It had just been a long time since we spent a Saturday together with the kids. Then I asked, 'Hey, while we are out, can I stop by a toy store? I need to buy some marbles.'"

CHAPTER SEVEN

Lemons, Lemons, Lemons

A Baptist deacon had advertised a cow for sale. "How much are you asking for it?" inquired a prospective purchaser. "One hundred and fifty dollars," said the Baptist deacon. Then the prospective purchaser asked how much milk she gave. The deacon answered, "Four gallons a day." The prospective purchaser questioned how he would know she would actually give that amount; and the deacon responded, "You can trust me. I'm a Baptist deacon." The other man said, "I'll take her. I'll take the cow home and bring you the money later. You can trust me; I'm a Methodist steward." When the deacon arrived home, he asked his wife what a Methodist steward was. "Oh," she replied, "a Methodist steward is about the same as a Baptist deacon." The deacon groaned, "Oh no, I've lost my cow."

We have all made some purchases in our lives. Some of them have been big, some small; some good, some bad; some important, some unimportant; but the fact is, if you make enough purchases, you will eventually get a lemon.

I remember the first lemon I purchased oh so well. It was a 1976 pick-up truck. I named it "Flattery" because it got me nowhere. I took it to a station for a ten-minute oil change, and the mechanic offered me some advice. He told me to keep the oil and change the truck. It was a lemon. It literally stayed in the repair shop more than on the road. My friends would only ride to school with me if I put them out 200 yards away because the truck back-fired so loud! It was embarrassing for them to be seen in it. Yes, this was my first lemon; but I assure you it was not my last.

The Bible says, "For ye are bought with a price: therefore glorify God in your body, and in your spirit, which are God's" (1 Corinthians 6:20). We, as Christians, were purchased with a price; and it is imperative we realize that price which was the precious blood of the Lord Jesus Christ. "Forasmuch as ye know that ye were not redeemed (purchased) with corruptible things, as silver and gold, from your vain conversation received by tradition from your fathers; But with the precious blood of Christ, as of a lamb without blemish and without spot" (1 Peter 1:18-19). I simply do not have the vocabulary to explain the vast price Jesus paid to purchase the children of God.

It breaks my heart to hear people speak or sing about the spilled blood of Jesus. It was not spilled! If you spill something, it is an accident or unintentional. Jesus' blood was shed intentionally! It was not spilled! He shed it to purchase us from death, hell, and the grave. Excuse me while I shout glory!

I believe you can agree with me that a great, grave price was paid to purchase your soul and mine. Therefore, I have some important questions for you. What did Jesus buy when He purchased you? Are you glorifying God in your body as the Scripture teaches, or did He purchase a lemon? I am very afraid we have churches that are running over with lemons.

A survey of churches in the United States revealed the following about church members:

10 percent cannot be found anywhere.

20 percent never attend a service.

25 percent admit they never pray.

35 percent admit they never read God's Word.

40 percent never contribute to the church or its missions.

60 percent never read or study the Bible lessons.

70 percent never attend the Sunday evening service.

75 percent never assume any responsibility in their church.

95 percent never win a soul to Christ.

But 100 percent expect to go to Heaven!

Let me share five characteristics of a lemon.

First, a lemon wants *Christ without commitment.* A humorous story that illustrates this well is the story of the girl who gave her boyfriend a picture of herself. She wrote on the back: "You are the love of my life. We are destined to be soulmates. I will love you forever and a day." Then she wrote: "P.S. If this relationship doesn't work out, I want my picture back." How well that illustrates the commitment of many to Christ. They want a relationship that is comfortable and convenient. But may I remind you that Christians are not called to comfort and convenience but to a cross and commitment. "If any man will come after me, let him deny himself, and take up his cross, and follow me" (Matthew 16:24).

While missionary David Livingstone was ministering in the jungles of Africa, he received a letter from friends that read: "We want to come and help if there are good roads to where you are." He wrote back and said, "I want people to come who will come even if there are no roads to where I am." He wanted committed people. A lemon wants Christ without commitment.

Secondly, a lemon wants *Christianity without change.* An elderly saint of God was on his deathbed and had a smile and look of anticipation on his face. A young man who was visiting him in ICU at the local hospital said, "I'd give the world to have what you have." The elderly saint responded, "That is just what you will have to do." We, as Christians, are to be different. "Therefore if any man be in Christ, he is a new creature: old things are passed away; behold, all things are become new" (2 Corinthians 5:17).

We are in this world in contact but not in conduct, and we are well assured we will never make a difference until we are different! We talk differently, walk differently, eat differently, dress differently, and go to different places than the world goes. I am convinced the church is too worldly and the world is too churchy. Most people want just enough of Jesus to get them out of hell but not enough of Jesus to get the hell out of them. Jesus wants to be "Lord of all, or He is not Lord at all." The church must get back to consecration, holiness, and Lordship if we are to impact our world for Christ. A lemon wants Christianity without change.

Thirdly, a lemon wants *showers of blessing without stewardship.* "Give, and it shall be given unto you . . ." (Luke 6:38). "Bring ye all the tithes into the storehouse, that there may be meat in mine house, and prove me now herewith, saith the LORD of hosts, if I will not open you the windows of heaven, and pour you out a blessing, that there shall not be room enough to receive it" (Malachi 3:10). Notice that stewardship takes place before the showers of blessings.

Every year when I speak on stewardship, someone always comes up and says, "I have a problem with this stewardship issue." The fact is I have found the problem is never a stewardship issue but an ownership issue. The Bible says, "The earth is the LORD's and the fulness thereof; the world, and they that dwell therein" (Psalm 24:1).

When an individual realizes 100 percent of what they have is loaned to them by God and they are a steward and not an owner, they will have no problem giving God His tithe of ten percent and more. Everything God controls gives. The sun gives the light of day. Plants give food. God the Father loved the world so much that He gave His only begotten Son, and Jesus Christ gave His life on Calvary's cross.

Does God have control of your life? I encourage you to look at two areas to determine an answer. They are your calendar and your checkbook. Look inside the checkbook of many church members, and here's what you will find: Mercedes payment, $800; vacation, $4000; poodle shampoo, $50; offering, $20; mission pledge, $5. "For where your treasure is, there will your heart be also" (Matthew 6:21). When your treasure is, spent on everything but the Kingdom of God, it is easy to see that your heart is not set on the things of God.

A family visited a church for the first time and was discussing their visit over Sunday lunch. The father said, "That preacher was horrible." The mother said she thought he was the worst she had ever heard. She also said the choir was appalling. They sounded like "dying ducks in a hail storm," she said. The daughter chimed in and said the musicians were obviously beginners because they were way off key. After a little time passed, the six-year-old son spoke up and said, "I thought it was a good show for the dollar we gave." A lemon wants showers of blessing without stewardship.

Fourthly, a lemon wants *serenity without surrender.* Lemons want to experience God's peace, but they also want to control what transpires. They are control freaks. Everything is fine as long as they can control the situation. They desire God's will as long as it is their will because ultimately they want to control their own lives and not allow God to have a part in it. But the Scripture teaches us it does not work that way!

"Be careful for nothing; but in every thing by prayer and supplication with thanksgiving let your requests be made known unto God. And the peace of God, which passeth all understanding, shall keep your hearts and minds through Christ Jesus" (Philippians 4:6-7). Did you notice we must make our prayers, supplications, and requests before we will experience the peace of God? There is no serenity without surrender. We must simply let go and let God. We must cast all our cares upon Him.

I love the story about the hitchhiker with a backpack who was picked up by a farmer in a pickup truck out in west Texas. The hitchhiker jumped in the back of the truck, and the farmer continued down the highway. After about five minutes, the farmer noticed the hitchhiker standing in the back of the truck loaded with his backpack. He pulled the truck over to the side of the highway, got out, and asked the hitchhiker why he did not take the backpack off and sit down. The hitchhiker said, "I didn't know if this truck could handle me and my backpack."

I know scores of people who wonder if God can handle them and their job, them and their finances, them and their relationships, them and their divorce, them and their sickness. I assure you He can if you just give it to Him. The Christian life is the only battle where victory is won through complete surrender. Don't be a lemon and want serenity without surrender. Let go and let God!

Fifthly, a lemon wants a *super place without self-involvement.* A lemon wants a great music program, a fabulous children's ministry, an awesome youth group, a thriving outreach ministry, a cutting-edge church — without any personal involvement. There is a sign on the wall in my home church in McMinnville, Tennessee, that asks a thought-provoking question: "If every member was just like me, what kind of church would this church be?" I encourage you to ask yourself that pertinent and powerful question.

Reverend Sam Jones from Cartersville, Georgia, was a powerful revivalist in the early 1900s. He had very successful revival services. A tradition of his on the last night was to have what he called a "Quitter's Night." People would bring to the altar the things they needed to quit. Men, for example, would bring their whiskey bottles, tobacco, and pictures of other men's wives. During one of these nights, a lady came to the altar and stayed there for quite some time. Rev. Jones knelt by her and asked what it was she needed to quit. She responded, "I ain't doing nothing for God, and I'm going to quit."

Our churches are full of people who are doing nothing for God. Their favorite song should be "I Shall Not Be Moved." They sing "Standing on the Promises," but all they do is "sit on the premises." They want a super place of worship without self-involvement.

A gymnast stretched a tightrope across a canyon and asked a group who were watching if they believed he could walk across and return safely. One lady quickly yelled, "I believe! I believe!" After he completed the walk, she said to the others: "I told you he could do it." He asked then if they believed he could push a wheelbarrow across that rope. The same lady screamed, "I believe! I believe!" Again, after successfully making the walk, the lady told the group: "I told you he could do it." Then he asked who believed he could put 150 pounds in the wheelbarrow and walk across the tightrope? The same lady bellowed, "I believe! I believe!" The gymnast looked at her and said, "Then you come and get in the wheelbarrow." With a petrified look on her face, she whispered, "I don't believe that much."

Many people say they have faith, but they never do any work for God. That is an oxymoron. The Bible says, "Even so faith, if it hath not works, is dead, being alone" (James 2:17). We are not saved to sit but to serve!

During the reign of Oliver Cromwell, the British government began to run low on silver coins. Lord Cromwell sent his men to the local cathedral to see if they could find any precious metal there. After investigating, they reported the only silver found were statues of the saints standing in the corners. The radical soldier and statesman of England said, "Good! We'll melt down the saints and put them in circulation!"

The church is in desperate need for revival. I am not talking about "working something up." I am talking about "praying something down." We need a Holy Ghost move of God to fall on the church that will build a fire in our hearts and melt away all of the gross impurities and sin in our lives. When we seek His face in personhood, He will give us His hand in provision.

Is a lemon good for anything? Certainly! You cannot make lemonade without it. But keep in mind, before you can make lemonade, the lemon must be broken. Before God can bless the church like He really desires to do, we must be broken before Him. "If my people, which are called by my name, shall humble themselves, and pray, and seek my face, and turn from their wicked ways; then will I hear from heaven, and will forgive their sin, and will heal their land" (2 Chronicles 7:14).

CHAPTER EIGHT

The Difference between Eagles and Chickens

Numbers 13:25-33

25. And they returned from searching of the land after forty days.

26. And they went and came to Moses, and to Aaron, and to all the congregation of the children of Israel, unto the wilderness of Paran, to Kadesh; and brought back word unto them, and unto all the congregation, and shewed them the fruit of the land.

27. And they told him, and said, We came unto the land whither thou sentest us, and surely it floweth with milk and honey; and this is the fruit of it.

28. Nevertheless the people *be* strong that dwell in the land, and the cities *are* walled, *and* very great: and moreover we saw the children of Anak there.

29. The Amalekites dwell in the land of the south: and the Hittites, and the Jebusites, and the Amorites, dwell in the mountains: and the Canaanites dwell

by the sea, and by the coast of Jordan.

30. And Caleb stilled the people before Moses, and said, let us go up at once, and possess it; for we are well able to overcome it.

31. But the men that went up with him said, We be not able to go up against the people; for they *are* stronger than we.

32. And they brought up an evil report of the land which they had searched unto the children of Israel, saying, The land, through which we have gone to search it, is a land that eateth up the inhabitants thereof; and all the people that we saw in it *are* men of a great stature.

33. And there we saw the giants, the sons of Anak, *which come* of the giants: and we were in our own sight as grasshoppers, and so we were in their sight.

There is a story about an American Indian who found an eagle's egg and placed it in the nest of a prairie chicken. The eaglet hatched with a brood of prairie chickens and grew up with them. Thinking he was a prairie chicken, the eagle did what the prairie chickens did. He clucked and he cackled. And because the prairie chickens never flew more than a few feet, neither did he.

One day the eagle saw a magnificent bird flying gracefully and effortlessly through the sky above him. The eagle asked the prairie chickens what that beautiful bird was. The prairie chickens said, "That's the eagle. He is the chief of birds, the monarch of the sky. But you could never fly like him because you are just a chicken."

The eagle never gave it a second thought. Eventually, he died

— deceived and deprived of his heritage because he was persuaded by the limited vision of others. God had designed him to soar in the heavens, but he scratched in the barnyard with the chickens. What a waste!

The greater waste is that millions of Christians, who are designed by the Creator to soar and accomplish awesome things for God, are scratching in the dirt for seeds and worms. Scores of people allow the vision of others to hold them captive and never reach their full potential for Christ. I believe Zig Ziglar was correct when he said, "Man was designed for accomplishment, engineered for success, and endowed with the seeds of greatness." God designed us to be eagles, not chickens! "But they that wait upon the LORD shall renew their strength; they shall mount up with wings as eagles; they shall run, and not be weary; and they shall walk, and not faint" (Isaiah 40:31).

In Numbers 13, God told Moses to pick one leader out of each of the twelve tribes of Israel to go and spy out the land of Canaan, then to report back to Moses their findings. After forty days of searching the land, they returned with two extremely different reports. Ten of the men came back and said, "The people are strong that dwell in the land; the cities have walls around them; and there are even giants there! There is no way we can take that land." They were chickens! But Joshua and Caleb came back with a far different observation. They said, "Let us go up at once and possess it, for we are able to overcome it." They were eagles! They knew God had referred to the land of Canaan 100 times up to this time as "the land . . . which I give . . ." (Numbers 13:2). God had promised it to them.

I recently saw a bumper sticker that read: "God said it, I

believe it, and that settles it." Well, that's not totally true. If God said it, that settles it — whether we believe it or not. We can rest on the promises of God.

Allow me to share four differences between eagles and chickens.

1. *An eagle sees possibilities, and a chicken sees problems.*
    The chickens saw the Amalekites, Hittites, Jebusites, Canaanites, and termites and said, "We can't handle them." They said, "We are like grasshoppers in their sight." Now do you honestly think the Amalekites looked at the Israelites and said, "You all are like grasshoppers in our sight?" Of course not! They said that about themselves! Always remember, we can never consistently perform in a manner that is inconsistent with how we view ourselves. What others say about you is not nearly as important as what you say about yourself. That is why the Bible says, ". . . let the weak say, I am strong" (Joel 3:10). The ten were chickens and saw only problems, but Joshua and Caleb saw possibilities. Do you constantly see problems or possibilities? Is your glass of water half empty or half full?

I love to tell the story of the two boys who were identical twins. One was a hope-filled optimist. "Everything is coming up roses," he would say. The other was a sad and hopeless pessimist. He thought Murphy, as in Murphy's Law, was an optimist. The worried parents of the boys took them to the local psychologist. The doctor suggested a plan to the parents to balance the twins' personalities. He suggested that on their next birthday they were to be put in separate rooms to open their presents. He said to give the pessimist the best toys they can afford and give the optimist a box of manure.

So on the next birthday, the parents followed the instructions and carefully observed the results. When they peeked in on the pessimist, they heard him complaining: "I don't like the color of this computer. I bet this calculator will break, and I don't like this game." Across the hall, they peeked in on the optimist. He was gleefully throwing manure up into the air giggling: "You can't fool me! With this much manure, there's gotta be a pony!"

2. *An eagle has great faith, and a chicken has great fear.*

Ten of the spies were scared to death. They saw giants and were chickens. Joshua and Caleb looked past the giants and saw God. They were eagles.

I encourage you to not let the giant of fear distort your view of God. The Bible says, "The LORD is my light and my salvation; whom shall I fear?" (Psalm 27:1). If you allow it, fear can paralyze you and keep you from becoming everything God wants you to be.

This reminds me of a story I heard about a couple in bed late one night. The husband was sound asleep until his wife jabbed him in his ribs saying, "Burt, wake up! There's a burglar downstairs." He had heard this so many times before. She repeated, "Burt, wake up!" "Okay, okay," he said as he tried to find his slippers, "I'm up." He grabbed his robe and stumbled down the stairs. When he reached the bottom step, he found himself staring into the barrel of a gun. "Hold it right there, buddy," a voice said firmly from behind the mask. "Show me where your valuables are." Burt did as he was told. When the burglar had his bag full, he began to leave; but Burt stopped him: "Wait. Before you go, could you please come up and meet my wife? She's been expecting you every night for over thirty years!"

I am convinced anytime we consider doing something for God there will be apprehension and fear. If there were not, it would just become mechanical. That type of fear is not sin; it is nature. But I also believe fear can become sin when it keeps us from doing that which God wants us to do. "Therefore to him that knoweth to do good, and doeth it not, to him it is sin " (James 4:17). Courage is not the absence of fear; it is going on in spite of your fear. John Wayne said, "Courage is being scared in your boots and saddling up anyway." Many people will never build the business, develop the relationship, teach the class, sing the song, or complete the project simply because of fear.

This story is a wonderful example of how fear can paralyze us from putting our faith in God and taking a risk. There were three turtles that were going out one summer afternoon for a country picnic. One carried a basket with the food; the second carried a jug of turtle-aid; and the third carried nothing. Once they arrived at the picnic area, they suddenly felt a drop of rain on their shells. "We can't have a picnic without an umbrella," said the first turtle. "Who will go back for one?" they asked. They made the choice that the empty-handed turtle would go back. "I won't go," he said. "As soon as I leave, you two will eat all the food and drink all the turtle-aid. I'll be cut out of everything!" "Wrong," the other two turtles said. "We'll wait for you — no matter how long you take." "No matter how long?" the third turtle asked. "No matter how long," they both replied. The third turtle turned back, and the others sat waiting. An hour, two hours, four, a day, two days, a week, two weeks all passed when one of the two turtles turned, looked at the other, and said, "Maybe we should go ahead and have the picnic." Suddenly, the voice of the third turtle came from within the bushes behind them saying: "If you do, I won't go!"

3. *An eagle focuses on triumph, and a chicken focuses on tragedy.*

I love the story of David and Goliath. One of my favorite parts are the words David said when he ran to face the giant: ". . . The LORD that delivered me out of the paw of the lion, and out of the paw of the bear, he will deliver me out of the hand of this Philistine" (1 Samuel 17:37). David focused on the triumphs God had brought him through and not the tragedies. I learned a long time ago that we could reflect on the scars or reach for the stars. The choice is up to us!

4. *An eagle sees the blessings, and a chicken sees the burdens.*

Two men looked out prison bars. One saw mud; the other saw stars. Do you see the blessings or the burdens of life? As Americans, we have so very much to be thankful for. Did you know one-third of the world is starving to death and two-thirds of our world goes to bed hungry every night? I recently learned forty percent of our world (two out of every five people) have no electrical service and sixty percent of the world have no phone service. Only three percent of the world's water supply is drinkable. Many times we are "grumbly hateful" when we should be "humbly grateful." Most of our praying is give or forgive; but we need to take some time to just say, "Thank you, Lord, for blessing me!"

Thank you, God, for dirty dishes; for they have a tale to tell.
While others may go hungry, we are eating very well.
With home, health, and happiness, we should not make a fuss.
By the stack of the evidence before us, God has been very good to us.

An account that is certainly beneficial to an attitude of gratitude is the story Jack Henton tells of leading music for a crusade on the island of Tobago, a leper colony. Henton said he noticed every night one particular lady would enter the tabernacle, immediately take her chair, and turn it around to face the back of the tabernacle instead of facing the pulpit. He thought to himself: *The nerve of this woman!* She not only did it one night but all four nights of the crusade. The last night Henton asked for song or hymn requests from the audience. With that, the lady turned around to face the pulpit and lifted her hand in the air. He said he could hardly believe his eyes. The lady had no fingers, no nose, and no ears because leprosy had eaten them off. He immediately felt sick to his stomach, and it was all he could do to ask her for her request which brought him to his knees: "Count Your Many Blessings." Henton led the congregation in the song, then ran outside, and began to sob. He was crying uncontrollably when a friend came to him and said, "Jack, you will never sing that song again, will you?" Henton said, "Yes, I will; but I will never sing it again the same way." An eagle sees the blessings, and a chicken sees the burdens.

CHAPTER NINE

In Order to Rise to the Top, You Must Get Off Your Bottom

Personal Motivation
Mark 10:46-52

46. And they came to Jericho: and as he went out of Jericho with his disciples and a great number of people, blind Bartimaeus, the son of Timaeus, sat by the highway side begging.

47. And when he heard that it was Jesus of Nazareth, he began to cry out, and say, Jesus, thou son of David, have mercy on me.

48. And many charged him that he should hold his peace: but he cried the more a great deal, Thou son of David, have mercy on me.

49. And Jesus stood still, and commanded him to be called. And they called the blind man, saying unto him, Be of good comfort, rise; he calleth thee.

50. And he, casting away his garment, rose, and came to Jesus.
51. And Jesus answered and said unto him, What wilt thou that I should do unto thee? The blind man said unto him, Lord, that I might receive my sight.
52. And Jesus said unto him, Go thy way; thy faith hath made thee whole. And immediately he received his sight, and followed Jesus in the way.

The name of our church's radio ministry is *Apples of Gold* taken from Proverbs 25:11, "A word fitly spoken is like apples of gold in pictures of silver." I am convinced there is great power in our words. The Bible says, "Death and life are in the power of the tongue" (Proverbs 18:21). Words can build us up or tear us down. Needless to say, words are powerful. I learned this principle at an early age.

As I said before, I did not meet my biological father until I was thirty years old. I was actually raised by two stepfathers. The first was not very good to me. He reminded me on a regular basis that I was very ignorant and never would amount to anything. To tell you the truth, I started believing him. That was the atmosphere and environment in which I was raised. Because of the constant criticizing, I began to assume I would always be a "nobody," work an insignificant job, and never amount to much of anything. I can still hear my stepfather telling me I was so stupid and I could not do anything right.

When I was sixteen, I received Jesus Christ as my personal Savior. That was the greatest decision I have ever made. At seventeen, I started preaching; and around the same time, I got a new stepfather who was a wonderful man. I loved him very deeply. I was busy preaching at rescue missions, nursing homes, jails, and anywhere else I was given the opportunity. One day my stepfather and I had a unique conversation. He asked me what I wanted to do with my life. I thought a little while and said I was working at Century as a janitor, mopping floors and cleaning toilets, and that I hoped to do a little preaching on the side. I will never forget what he said to me then: "You can be so much more, Benny! God has gifted you. You are extremely intelligent! You ought to go to Bible college, receive your training, and enter into full-time ministry." He went on to say, "Every degree that you complete, I will pay for." Honestly, I was scared to death! Could I do it? Was I really smart enough? Was I really ignorant? I still don't know if I believed in myself, but the motivating force was that he believed in me.

I wonder how many people stop because so few say go. I am thrilled to report to you that my stepfather did pay for four degrees: my Associate's, my Bachelor's, my Master's, and my Doctor's degrees. The lowest grade I ever made was a ninety-four. What was the difference in my elementary years and my college years? I was motivated because I had someone who believed in me! Motivation is powerful!

It is encouraging to me to know that God has a plan and purpose for each of our lives. "For I know the thoughts that I think toward you, saith the LORD, thoughts of peace, and not of evil, to give you an expected end" (Jeremiah 29:11). There is no doubt that God had a beautiful plan for blind Bartimaeus' life. God's plan was to restore his sight, but Bartimaeus had a part in that plan.

A humorous story that illustrates this point is the account of a young man who took a short cut home late one night through the cemetery. While walking, he fell into an open grave. He called, he prayed, and he tried to climb out but to no avail. There was no one around to hear his cries or lend him a hand. So he settled down for the night in a corner of the dark grave to await morning. A little while later, another person went the same route and fell into the same grave. He started clawing and screaming for help just as the first man had done. Suddenly, an exhausted, depressed moan came from the corner of the grave saying, "You can't get out of here." Needless to say, the second man did! He got motivated! Yes, God has a part but so do we. We are laborers together with God. Without God, we cannot; without us, He will not.

Notice the five steps that motivated Bartimaeus to accomplish his mission in life. These steps will work in your life, too.

1. *Assume responsibility for your mission.*
The Bible says in Mark 10:47, ". . . he began to cry out. . . ." Bartimaeus knew there were a lot of people in Jericho that day; however, he was responsible for getting the attention of Jesus. When are you going to quit holding everyone else responsible for where you are in life? Friend, if you have "ring around the collar," don't blame Maytag, Tide, Purex, or your wife. Wash your neck! Take responsibility for where you are in life, and quit blaming everyone else! I realize your third grade teacher gave everyone else a cookie but you, and that's why your life has turned out the way it has; but it is time to move on and take responsibility for where you are. Robert Schuller was correct when he said, "If it is to be, it is up to me."

2. *Believe you can through God.*

Bartimaeus said, and I am paraphrasing, "I want to receive my sight." I am convinced we can do great things through Jesus Christ. I remember years ago traveling to a college to speak to a group of professors. I felt so inadequate. I literally felt like a penny waiting for change. In desperation, I finally said to God, "What can a country boy like me teach these intellectual, well-educated professors?" God responded, "You can't teach them anything, but I can teach them volumes through you." I encourage you to believe you can through God. Henry Ford was right when he said, "Whether you say you can or you can't, you are right."

> *If you think you are beaten, you are.*
> *If you think you dare not, you don't.*
> *If you like to win but you think you can't,*
> *It's almost certain you won't.*
> *Life's battles don't always go*
> *To the stronger or faster man;*
> *But sooner or later, the one who wins*
> *Is the one who thinks he can!*

3. *Stop worrying about what other people think.*

The people in Jericho told Bartimaeus to "just keep quiet." Did he? No! "... he cried the more ..." (Mark 10:48). I am not saying that what people think and say about us are not important. However, what I am saying is there are people who are critical by nature. There is no way you will ever be able to please them.

I recently read some interesting stats in the book *The People Skills of Jesus.* Twenty-five percent of your acquaintances don't like you and never will. Another twenty-five percent don't like you but could be persuaded to like you under the right circumstances. Another twenty-five percent like you but could easily be persuaded to dislike you. The last twenty-five percent like you and will stand by you no matter what you do.

I love to express this last point by telling the story about the grandfather, grandson, and the donkey who were making a trip to town. They started by letting the boy ride the donkey and the grandfather walk beside them. Some people who were watching said, "Look at that selfish child making that poor old man walk, while he rides." Upon hearing this, the grandfather and grandson switched places, making the child walk and the grandfather ride. Further along the route, other people who were watching said, "Look at that old man making that precious little child walk, while he rides." Upon hearing this, they both started riding the donkey. Then the people said, "How cruel for both of them to place that heavy load on that donkey!" By the time they arrived in town, the grandfather and the grandson were carrying the donkey!

Bill Cosby was correct when he said, "I don't know the secret to success; but I do know the secret to failure, and that is trying to please everybody." Stop worrying about what others will say!

4. *Stop waiting for ideal circumstances.*

There were a lot of people crowding around Jesus on this day in Jericho. It probably was not the best time and place for Bartimaeus to approach Him, but he did anyway. Scores of people are waiting for all of the conditions to be right before they start on their mission. I have got news for them. Everything will never be just right! The Bible says, "He that observeth the wind shall not sow; and he that regardeth the clouds shall not reap" (Ecclesiastes 11:4).

I have heard couples say, "We are going to have a baby when we can afford it." If you wait until you can afford a child, you will never have one. "We are going to buy a house when we can afford it." There again, you will never own a house if you wait until you can afford it. "I am going to enter the ministry when everything is right." If you wait until every condition is right to enter the ministry, you never will!

This poem says it best:

> *The bride, bent with age, leaned over her cane*
> *Her steps uncertain, needed guiding;*
> *While down the church aisle with a warm, toothless smile*
> *The groom in his wheelchair gliding.*
> *And who is the elderly couple thus wed?*
> *You'll find when you closely explore it*
> *That is this rare, most conservative pair*
> *Who waited until they could afford it.*

5. *Get started now.*

The word *procrastination* comes from the Latin word meaning "belonging to the morrow." Procrastination will prolong you from getting started on your mission. It will keep you focused on tomorrow. I have learned that "one of these days" is usually "none of these days."

The problem with many of us is we are controlled by our feelings, not the facts. "I don't feel like getting started." Well, feelings are fickle! Did you know you are more apt to act yourself into a feeling than feel yourself into an action? Yes, motivation follows action and not vice versa. I have heard people say, "I am going on a diet when I get motivated." (Be careful of diets; take off the "t," and look what you get!) No, you won't get motivated. You take action, go on the diet, lose five or ten pounds, and then you will get motivated. Get moving!

Will Rogers said, "Even if you are on the right track, if you don't move, you will get run over." No matter what, you must get started! Don't say, "If I start college now, I will be forty when I graduate." Think: "How old will I be if I don't go?" (You will still be forty!) Get started!

I believe eighty percent of success is getting started. Once a person is motivated to start, they become a powerful force.

I love to tell the story about the army private who pulled KP duty. After twelve hours of peeling potatoes, he came back to the barracks exhausted. He was so bone tired that he could barely manage to drop his worn body onto the bed. He didn't even bother taking off his clothes. As he rolled over to catch some much needed sleep, he noticed a letter from his girlfriend. He quickly opened it and read, "Dear John, if I could feel your strong, masculine arms embrace me one more time or taste your sweet, tender lips just one more time, I know it could continue. I know I could be true to you, but . . . ." John didn't bother reading another word. He jumped from the bed and took off running. He forgot how fatigued he was. This man was on a mission. John was running off the military post, doing the 100 in about 9.5. When he reached the guardhouse, the guard on duty took out his M-14 rifle and aimed it right at John's heart. He told him to halt or he would shoot. John never broke stride which left the guard no option. The very last words John uttered were these: "My mother is in heaven; my father is in hell; and my girl is in Chicago. I am going to see one of them tonight." Motivation can be a powerful force.

What is the mission God has for your life? Are you doing it? Are you working toward it?

Florence Littauer tells a powerful story about the importance of pursuing one's mission in life. It is about her mother-in-law Marita Littauer. After knowing her mother-in-law for many years and being a little intimidated by her, one day Florence asked the aging woman what she would have been if she could have been anything she wanted. Marita answered without hesitation: "An opera singer. I wanted to study music; but my parents felt that was a waste of time, that I would make more money in the millinery business." She continued, "I was in one show in college, and I had the lead." The memory of that dream never left Marita Littauer — even though her mother had shot it down. In her last days, her mind faded and she could no longer speak. But some evenings, while in the nursing home where she lived, the nurses said she would stand by her chair and sing beautiful opera. Even in the twilight of her years, that deep desire never left her. Florence said, "Mother had a talent that never developed; a music box that was never allowed to play; a career that was never begun. Mother died with the music still in her."

Friend, you have only one life. It will soon be past, and only what is done for Christ will last. One day we will look back on our life and say one of two things: Either I am glad I did, or I wish I had. I hope you can say *I am glad I did.*

For more information or to contact Dr. Benny Tate you may write to:

> Dr. Benny Tate
> Rock Springs Congregational Methodist Church
> 219 Rock Springs Road
> Milner, GA 30257

or telephone:

> 770.229.8663

or log on the church's website at:

> www.rockspringsonline.com